THE 14 DAYS OF CHRISTMAS

LOUISE BAY

Published by Louise Bay 2021

ISBN – 978-1-910747-797

BOOKS BY LOUISE BAY

The Mister Series

Mr. Mayfair

Mr.Knightsbridge

Mr. Smithfield

Mr. Park Lane

Mr. Bloomsbury

The 14 Days of Christmas

This Christmas

Player Series

Private Player

International Player

Standalones

Hollywood Scandal

Love Unexpected

Hopeful

The Empire State Series

Gentleman Series

The Wrong Gentleman

The Ruthless Gentleman

The Royals Series

The Earl of London

The British Knight

Duke of Manhattan

Park Avenue Prince

King of Wall Street

The Nights Series

Indigo Nights

Promised Nights

Parisian Nights

Faithful

Sign up to the Louise Bay mailing list at
www.louisebay/mailinglist

Read more at www.louisebay.com

ONE

Sebastian

Last time I checked, I wasn't Santa Claus and this wasn't a public holiday, which meant there was nothing to explain the Christmas music blasting through my office door. I took a deep breath and tried to unclench my jaw. Did people give up working for the entire month of December? Didn't they know I was in a meeting, and they should be doing their jobs?

"I need a breakdown by end of business tomorrow," I said to Ali as the image on Luke's jumper caught my attention. Reindeer? Really? My head of compliance was usually so reliable.

"Don't you fly out tonight?" Ali asked.

I didn't reply. I wasn't sure what me taking a plane to Barbados had to do with anything.

"Yes of course, I can get you that breakdown," she spluttered, rifling through her note pad.

"Good, then that's everything." I stood and everyone scooped up their papers and headed out in silence—my preferred background noise for the office. Rather than Mariah Carey or Wham! or Michael bloody Bublé.

As I opened my office door, there was no mistaking the dulcet tones of Slade wishing me a Merry Christmas. I stalked to the outer office where my assistant sat.

"Get. Them. To. Turn. It. Off," I said through gritted teeth.

"People are just happy, Sebastian," she said on a sigh. "But yes, I'll ask them to turn it down."

"No reason for them to be any happier now than they were last month. Or the month before that." I couldn't tell what got me more irritated—the idiocy of the Christmas season, or my rage at the idiocy of the Christmas season. "Is that . . . tinsel around your screen?" I asked, incredulous. What was it about this time of year that sent everybody sideways? Made people wear terrible clothing, listen to terrible music, and eat too much terrible food? I couldn't wait to leave the country and escape it all. Just a few more hours and I'd be headed to a Caribbean beach. One of my oldest friends, Griffin, was due to fly out to join me for a couple of days, but apart from that I'd be blissfully alone.

My mobile vibrated on my desk, and I headed back into my office to see who it was. I accepted the call. "Granny?" She never called me in the week.

"Sebastian. I need your help."

My pulse thudded low in my eardrums and I sent up a silent prayer that nothing was wrong. There was no one more important to me than Granny. I called her every weekend and she came to stay with me several times a year, and we'd stay up drinking too much whiskey, swearing, and putting the world to rights. She'd been a guiding force for me growing up, more of a parent to me than my mum and dad. She was the one person I trusted more than anyone in the world, the one person I'd do anything for—no questions asked.

"What can I do?" I asked.

"I've sprained my ankle and—"

Why wouldn't she just come and live with me as I'd asked her to a hundred times before? "I'm sending a car to bring you back to London."

"Don't be ridiculous. I'm not coming to London."

"I'll send a nurse to you—"

"Sebastian, I'm seventy-three years old. I'm pretty sure I've earned the right not to be interrupted when I speak."

No one on this earth could get away with talking to me like that. No one except Granny. "Sorry. What do you need?"

"The doctor told me that I have to keep my ankle elevated and can't put any weight on it."

Sounded like good advice.

"We're in the second week of December. The Snowsly Christmas market is due to open in three days and we're not nearly prepared. I've not even finished putting up the decorations in the Manor."

"I'm sure you don't need to worry about Snowsly. And get the reception staff to put up the Manor decorations." Granny had a small hotel in the Cotswold village of Snowsly. She had a manager in there these days but she liked to keep busy, bossing everyone around.

"The village relies on me. You know I chair the Christmas committee. Even in the two days since I sprained my ankle—"

"You're only calling *now* when you sprained your ankle two days ago? Why am I the last to hear?"

"Me and my ankle are going to be fine. That's not my concern. The problem is that by the time I've recovered,

Christmas will be over and so might some of the villagers' livelihoods if we don't pull off a Christmas to remember. The shopkeepers in the village make most of their money in the run-up to Christmas. I need you to come to Snowsly and be my eyes and ears. There's only so much I can do, sitting on my sofa."

"Come to Snowsly?" I was hours away from a first-class flight to the Caribbean, where Christmas was almost forgotten. The last thing I wanted to do was change my plans and head to Christmas *headquarters* in the heart of England.

"You know how much the village businesses rely on the custom they get at the Christmas market."

I *did* know, but only because I'd heard it from her. I'd never actually seen Christmas in Snowsly with my own eyes. Since I was eighteen years old, I'd always spent the holiday season on the beach or by the pool, somewhere far away from the madness of Christmas. It was ludicrous how people abandoned their sanity in December, pretending they were having such a marvelous time. And why? No one had ever adequately explained it to me. I much preferred the reality of a margarita by the pool, guaranteed sunshine, and no mention of the festive season.

"I'm sure everyone will be just fine. Do you want me to send someone up?"

"No, Sebastian." I could count on one hand the number of times Granny seemed to lose patience with me, and based on her exasperated sigh, this was one of them. "Everyone won't be fine and no, I don't want you to send any of your poor staff up who, no doubt, have their own Christmas crises to deal with. I need you to come up and help. I wouldn't ask if it wasn't important."

I sighed. I wasn't going to say no to her. I couldn't. There wasn't anything I wouldn't do for Granny. It was just that if the powers of hell had devised a bespoke way of torturing me, making me go to Snowsly to organize Christmas was about as bad as it could get. I'd take having my fingernails ripped out, being forced to cross a crocodile-infested river, or even flying economy before I'd endure a Christmas in England. Especially a Christmas in Snowsly. There was nowhere more festive.

THE CAR WOUND its way up and down hills, through the narrow, winding roads that joined each small village and hamlet of the Cotswolds in a lumpy web of picturesque England. Nothing and no one traveled anywhere quickly around here.

The roads had been designed for horses, not cars, and so at least half of any journey between villages was spent with two wheels in a ditch, waiting for an oncoming car to tentatively inch forward, the centimeter of space between cars the difference between onward travel and an insurance claim. In summer the roads were long, green tunnels, made of the branches of the trees on each side interlocking above as if joining hands in some kind of three-hundred-year-old country dance. The sides of the tree-tunnels were lined with hedgerows, bursting with nuts, berries, and the animals that feasted on them. At the end of each tunnel waited the reward of a guaranteed spectacular view of farm or woodland. Some vistas stretched across to the distant blue-grey shadows of the Malvern Hills.

Now, in the throes of winter, the hedgerows were bare and the branches of the trees stretched across the road like skeletons, trying unsuccessfully to block out the white winter sky.

The next pretty village looked a lot like the last—the inevitable bright red postbox somewhere in the center, contrasting with the local yellow Cotswold stone walls and higgledy-piggledy houses from every era of the last thousand years. The pub. The church. The dog walker, wrapped up from head to foot in wool and tweed. And the hint here and there that we were in the month of madness—wreaths on doors, lights around windows, decorated trees in front gardens. Insanity.

It had been a long time since I'd made it to this part of the world, but I found I still knew it as well as my bedroom ceiling. For the last decade or so, I'd sent my driver to bring Granny to London to stay with me. It saved me time and she enjoyed the break. I didn't often leave London, unless it was to go abroad. What was the point? London had everything I needed. The recruitment business I'd worked tirelessly to create. The penthouse that overlooked the Thames. The life I'd built for myself.

Being back in the Cotswolds was like stepping back into my childhood. I'd spent every summer navigating the hills that surrounded Snowsly. Foraging in the hedgerows, getting lost in the maize fields, being a kid with no worries. Every summer. Every Easter. Every school holiday.

Except Christmas.

"This is it, Bradley," I said to the driver as we turned into High Street. Snowsly was one of the bigger villages in the Cotswolds. As well as the obligatory pub—two, in fact— and post box, it had a number of shops located around the village green, all popular with tourists and locals alike. Tea rooms that opened for breakfast and lunch only, a restaurant. And the Manor.

"The Manor is right at the top of the hill," I said to Bradley.

Granny bought the Manor before my grandfather died and before I was born. It had been a number of years since she actively ran it. I convinced her she needed a manager in the place a few years before. But that didn't mean she didn't have her nose in most things. And it didn't mean she wasn't still running the village. Granny couldn't sit back. I'd gotten the trait from her.

We drove past the village green—the place where I played cricket every summer and hunted for Easter eggs in spring, where Granny would drag me to watch the local children dance around the maypole on May Day. Now, in the maypole's place stood a large Christmas tree, lit up with thousands of gold lights. The edge of the green was circled with beech trees adorned with more lights.

Even I had to admit it looked pretty.

We pulled up in front of the Manor and I got out, my expensive, inappropriate shoes crunching in the snow.

How ironic.

As a child, seeing Snowsly in the snow at Christmastime was all I'd wanted. It was as if the place had been built for the season. I'd been convinced that all the village needed to make it perfect was a sprinkle of ice and snow.

Then it would be Narnia.

Now, over a decade after my last trip here, my childhood fantasy had come true. I tipped my head back to take in the four stories of windows set into the yellow stone of the Manor. I'd known every inch of this place growing up. It had been my sanctuary. My safe haven. The place I'd felt most like myself. And even now, there was something comforting about it. Not as comforting as a first-class seat to Barbados, but comforting all the same.

"Sebastian?"

I snapped my head toward the sound of my name and

smiled. "Mary. Good to see you." I bent and placed a kiss on Granny's housekeeper's cheek. She looked exactly the same as the last time I'd seen her—big bosomed and not to be messed with, like some nineteen fifties matron. I knew that inside, she was pure marshmallow.

"I finally get to see you at Christmas," she said. "I have the Blue Room made up for you."

I might not have been here for a long time, but I knew enough to know the Blue Room was the best in the house. "Are you sure it's not booked for guests? I'm happy to stay in the Green Room." The Green Room had a single bed and was so small you couldn't swing a cat in it, but I knew my Granny would rather cancel Christmas than accept money from me, so I'd rather I wasn't depressing takings.

"We're fully booked apart from the Blue Room." Mary's tone was clipped and not to be argued with.

"I can't wait," I replied, taking a small case from Bradley. I'd decanted the things from my Barbados case that could be used in Snowsly, and Bradley would take the rest back. Cotswold-appropriate clothing would follow by courier tomorrow. I was pretty sure I was going to need more than sunglasses and swimming trunks to get me through the next couple of weeks.

"Let me take that." Mary yanked my case out of my hand. "You need to get to the committee meeting. It starts in three minutes."

Granny was clearly still ruling the roost with an iron fist.

I took the case back. "Then I'll have to take the stairs two at a time," I said. There was no way I was letting Mary take my case for me. I wasn't a guest. I was here for Granny.

And I'd be gone by Christmas Eve.

TWO

Celia

The adrenaline coursing through my veins made my legs bounce, the panic chased fluttery breaths from my chest while nausea swirled in my stomach. Every second we weren't doing something was time wasted. I swallowed and pulled my mouth into a smile.

Christmas in Snowsly this year was going to be the best yet. It just had to be.

A lot could be accomplished in two days. As long as no one else sprained their ankle or broke their leg or the village Christmas tree didn't fall down.

I glanced around at the Snowsly Christmas committee and zipped the small gold "C" on the chain around my neck back and forth. Then I surreptitiously crossed my fingers. A little luck couldn't hurt, could it?

"Celia, uncross your fingers and leave that necklace alone. Everything's going to be fine," Ivy barked. She might have sprained her ankle but there was nothing wrong with her eyesight.

"I know," I lied, nodding.

"Ahh, here he is," she said, a grin filling her face as if Santa himself had appeared in the doorway. "Most of you know my grandson, Sebastian."

I turned to see a tall, suited man with a serious expression stalk toward Ivy and plant a kiss on her cheek.

"Come and sit by me," Ivy said and she started to shuffle across her sofa.

"If you move, then I'll be straight back to London," he said through a smile. His voice was like thick cream poured over chocolate yule log—rich and silky. I made a mental note to buy the ingredients this week to make the festive treat. "The doctor has told you to rest. That's why I'm here, after all."

"Sebastian, young man. Good to have you here. It's been a while," Jim said, half standing, his usual floral shirt covered with one of my favorite of his Christmas jumpers: a green sweat shirt with a picture of his grandkids dressed up as elves on the front. Jim, the village florist, had a different Christmas jumper for each day of December.

"Too long," Sebastian said, shaking Jim's hand. "I'm here to work and don't want to interrupt. What's on the agenda?"

Every now and then I'd heard people talk about Ivy's grandson, who used to visit Snowsly often as a child, but I'd never met Sebastian before. When Ivy said she was going to get him to come up and help, I'd expected a teenager with overgrown hair sporting a t-shirt featuring a band I'd never heard of. The last thing I'd been expecting was a . . . man. A man so tall he had to duck under the doorframe when he walked in. A man in an expensive-looking suit and a face that belonged more on the big screen than the back living room of a small hotel in the middle of England.

The first man I'd noticed since my boyfriend had left me.

"Celia?" Ivy prompted. "What's next?"

I almost jumped as she interrupted my appreciation of her grandson. "Priority for tomorrow are the market stalls—or huts or miniature German houses, whatever you want to call them. They're being erected on the village green. The company we're renting from can't supply as many people to put them up as usual, so we'll need to provide reinforcements. Also we need to finish getting the decorations up in the Manor—I'm going to try to do that tonight." My phone buzzed in my hand and I tried to ignore it but when I glanced down at the screen, I could see the company we were renting the stalls from calling. "Sorry, I have to get this."

I tried to keep my breathing even as I listened to Bruce tell me how there was not only a shortage of people coming tomorrow to set up the stalls, but a shortage of stalls, too. "Thanks for letting me know," I said. "We'll see you tomorrow."

"What is it?" Ivy asked.

"Nothing I can't handle," I replied, smiling as if it was no problem at all to source additional lookalike alpine huts. Where would I start? Maybe pull a couple out of my cleavage or from the back of my wardrobe. Surely if Bruce was short, it meant there was a supply issue all over.

"We're all in this together," Keely, the always immaculate art-gallery owner said. "What happened?"

I took a deep breath and shook my head. "We're going to be two short on Christmas stalls. But it's fine. I'll figure something out."

"We've had to tell the Christmas Shop they can only have one stall as it is," Keely said. "How are we going to tell two other stores they can't take part in the market? The market brings in twenty percent of my entire year's sales. I know it's the same for the other shops in the village."

"We're all aware of how important the Christmas market is to the village," Ivy said. "That's why we're all here. That's why Sebastian has cancelled his trip to Barbados to be here. Snowsly is synonymous with Christmas and *the* destination for people looking to celebrate the lead-up to Christmas. Nothing's going to change that."

My smile was fixed in place. It wouldn't do to panic. Things would start to spiral and that was going to happen over my dead body. "There's a solution," I said. "An easy fix. Just leave it with me." I hadn't thought if it yet, but I knew I'd come up with something. I had to.

"Maybe Sebastian could help," Ivy said.

"Happy to be of assistance with any hut crisis that comes along," he said.

I wasn't sure if he was being sarcastic or genuine. I glanced up a him and he offered me a tight smile and for a second my mind wandered and I wondered what he used on his hair to get it looking that shiny.

"Yes," I said, pulling myself back to the moment. "Christmas stalls should be a priority for everyone tomorrow." I glanced between Howard and Barbara, who were sitting either side of Ivy and Sebastian. I was trying to avoid looking directly at him, like making eye contact would cause me to burst into flames. "We need to get them up and we need to get them decorated. Everything needs to be perfect for the opening of the Christmas market in two days." I had to get out of this meeting so I could figure out what to do, because I was pretty sure my boobs or my wardrobe weren't going to produce a solution. "I suggest we focus on that and meet back here again tomorrow at six. In the meantime, I'll source some additional huts and decorate Snowsly Manor." I was sure that as soon as I started decorating the Manor, a creative solution to the lack of stalls would come to me. Then we'd be back on track to having the best Christmas in Snowsly history.

"Sebastian can help Celia decorate the Manor this evening, can't you, Sebastian?" Ivy asked.

Sebastian cleared his throat. "Whatever you need, Granny."

"No need," I said. "I can get it done."

"Two pairs of hands will mean you're home and tucked in bed early. Sebastian should definitely help," Keely said, glancing at Peter.

"I agree," Peter said. "We all need a good night's sleep when we've got such a busy day ahead of us."

I glanced up at Keely and then Peter. Why did they care if I had help decorating the tree? And if they did, why didn't they offer their own assistance?

"Like I said," Sebastian said. "I'm happy to help."

"Great!" I said, not entirely meaning it. I needed to think straight and come up with solutions. I could already feel Sebastian's presence blurring my focus, and that's the last thing I needed. "I've pulled all the decorations out of storage, so I'll show you what we need to do."

The meeting dispersed, leaving just Ivy, Sebastian, and me in the sitting room.

"I'll leave you two to catch up," I said, "and make a start on the decorations."

"No, no, no," Ivy said, waving her walking stick in my general direction. "We've got plenty of time for catching up. We need decorations. Sebastian, go on with Celia and help her, if you would."

Sebastian nodded and I led the way into the the reception area, where the decorations were all waiting. Life couldn't get any better than decorating for Christmas, with an endless soundtrack of festive music piped through the reception speakers. Unless two extra Christmas market huts magicked their way onto the green overnight.

"Thank you for agreeing to help," I said. "But I have to insist on having the final *sleigh* on the placement of decorations." I beamed up at him, delighted at my joke, but his face didn't register a glimmer of a smile. I was going to have to up my pun game.

I waved to Eve behind the reception desk, a phone tucked under her ear as she typed on the computer in front of her. She smiled, then her eyes slid to Sebastian and her cheeks bloomed pink. I glanced at Sebastian to find he wasn't even looking at Eve. He'd spotted the boxes of overspilling decorations by the desk. Apparently, he could make a grown woman blush just by being in the same room as her.

It was hardly surprising. Now he was standing next to me, it was even more obvious how very tall he was. And his dark hair was just starting to curl at the ends . . . I had to stop myself from reaching up to feel how the glossy strands felt between my fingers.

I placed my palms on my cheeks, trying to register the heat factor on my own face. I'd just have to pretend it was windchill.

"I bet you're excited to be in Snowsly for Christmas," I said, keeping my gaze on the tree. If I didn't look at him, I wouldn't notice how handsome he was. It was unlikely to work, and I'd probably have to sacrifice sleep tonight to find a solution to the hut crisis. Sebastian wasn't easy to ignore. "Ivy hasn't stopped talking about how *yule* be home for Christmas."

"Snowsly isn't home." He sounded like I'd told him he looked a little overdressed in his deliciously well-cut suit, rather than made one of the all-time best Christmas puns I'd ever thought up. It was some of my best work. Maybe he was tired?

"What do you do?" I asked, trying to get him to open up a little. He seemed rather stiff.

"I own my own recruitment business."

That sounded impressive, though I wasn't sure what to say in response. I settled on, "That must be fun." I bent to figure out what had been pulled out of storage. "Oh, look." I pulled open the cardboard box full of the Snowsly Annual Christmas decorations. "This is like leafing through Snowsly's Christmas history." Each year, Keely designed a Christmas decoration for the Christmas tree on the green. Ivy placed the ornament on the tree every year at the opening of the Christmas market. A couple of years ago, we'd started to sell replicas at select market stalls. I pulled out a glass snowman bauble. "2018. A lovely one. So festive." I placed it back in his cardboard holder. "2019 was my favorite though." I scanned the decorations, lifting corners of tissue paper, trying to find the glittery elf that encapsulated Christmas for me—he was merry and bright and everything that Christmas should be.

"Shall we focus on the present rather than the past?" Sebastian asked from behind me.

I grinned, delighted at his joke. "I like what you did there. I get it—Christmas *present*. I love a good Christmas pun."

He gave me a look like I'd completely lost my baubles. "I can assure you that I will never make an intentional Christmas pun. Not ever."

"Oh Sebastian," I said, sad for him. "How much you

miss." I exhaled. "Anyway, you're right. We need to get on. I'm just being sentimental because these are a beautiful reminder of happier—I mean, happy times." I had to focus on the good stuff. Not every Christmas would be ruined just because last year had been so difficult.

Sebastian didn't respond. He just stared at the boxes, his mouth set into a hard line and a sadness in his eyes I didn't understand.

"Let's start with the tree," I said, pulling out the over-sized red duffle bag. "So . . . where is home if Snowsly isn't it for you?" I asked.

"London."

"Oh, I've not been to see the decorations there in forever," I replied. "The Bond Street lights are always my favorite. What's the theme this year?"

He frowned. "How would I know?"

I had to force my smile a little. How could he not know? "Ahhh, I bet you do all your Christmas shopping online. I like to go out to the shops and drink in the atmosphere, but you must be very busy running your own company."

Sebastian sighed, ignoring my invitation to elaborate. "The tree is in this bag? It's big enough to store a couple of corpses."

"What a unique way to measure volume," I said, giving him a sideways glare. "Perhaps you could investigate another storage solution for any bodies you may have. We reuse this bag every year."

The corners of his mouth twitched. Finally! He did have a sense of humor, but one suited to jokes about murder rather than puns about Christmas.

"Lucky for us the lights are all on the tree, so we just have to do the fun stuff."

Sebastian snorted and his stern expression replaced any hint of a smile. "None of this is fun."

"What do you mean?" I unzipped the bag and dragged out the bottom third of an artificial tree. The ones either side of the entrance were potted and real, but it was much easier to keep reception neat and tidy if needles weren't falling on the floors constantly. And then there was the incident with a resident's dog the year before last that no one wanted to relive. "We get to put on the baubles, the felt reindeer, the candy canes. We get to arrange them all and make everything look perfect. We're going to have a whole mountain of fun." We just needed the scent of mulled wine and mince pies and I'd be in Christmas heaven.

"Doesn't the incessant Christmas music drive you completely crazy?" Sebastian asked as I passed him the plug for the lights on the tree, which he put into the socket I indicated by the side of the reception desk.

"Crazy happy?" I asked. "I've been known to sneak on a bit of Bublé's Christmas album as early as August."

He rolled his eyes. "What's next?" he said, glancing between the duffel bag and the stand I'd placed on the floor at the bottom of the stairs. The light from the windows would make sure the baubles glittered day and night. It was going to be spectacular.

"The bottom of the tree needs to go in first." I strained to lift it before Sebastian, getting the gist of what was going on, pulled it from my arms and unceremoniously dumped it into the stand. "Right. Thank you."

"Next section?" he asked.

"I learned my lesson last year that you need to fluff *before* plugging in the next piece of trunk."

"Excuse me?" Sebastian said.

"Like this," I said, pulling down the branches and fluffing them up so they came to life. Almost.

Sebastian sighed and began working on the other side of the tree.

"You know, you might find it more comfortable if you changed out of your suit." Presumably he had a change of clothes. He looked a little out of place in such formal attire.

"And into my Christmas jumper?" He nodded toward the cardigan I was wearing, which was my second-favorite Christmas jumper. It had Christmas puddings on each of the pockets and the buttons were tiny Christmas wreaths. It had held the number-one slot until last September, when I'd found the most darling jumper, which had a circle of reindeer around the hem, looking into the night sky. The rest of the jumper was covered in stars that actually lit up. I was saving it for Christmas Eve. Maybe I'd actually get to wear it this year for the first time.

"Absolutely" I said. "I can hold the fort here while you change if you like."

He rolled his eyes and I winced. He'd been joking. "I'm good. Can we slot the next section in?"

I glanced at his side of the tree. It wasn't quite how it needed to be. "Hmmm, just a second," I said, shuffling around the tree. "Why don't you check my side and I'll do yours. Two pairs of eyes are better than one."

"Your side looks fine," he said, barely even glancing at it. I ignored him and started to re-fluff his side. As I moved past him, I breathed in his scent. He might not be in the best mood but at the same time he was built like Adonis and smelled just like Christmas—all fresh-cut pine and crackling fires. He might just be the perfect man. If only he liked Michael Bublé. And was a little more . . . festive.

"There," I said, standing back, dipping to different

angles to make sure I'd covered all the holes. "I think we're done."

"Finally." He lifted the next section and slotted it in. "Now, let me guess. We fluff this big guy's trunk?"

Big guy? "The branches," I corrected him. "So how come I've not seen you in Snowsly before?" I asked as I worked my fingers through the branches.

"Busy. Ivy comes to London to visit."

"This must be so much fun for you then," I said, grinning up at him as he lifted the final section of the tree like it was nothing more than one of the baubles we were about to hang. Strong, handsome, smelled like Christmas. What did he have to be grumpy about? He snapped the last bit of the tree into place and all three sections lit up. Instantly the reception area looked more festive.

The familiar opening bars of "Last Christmas" spilled through the hotel lobby and my stomach began to churn. I didn't want to think about this time last year.

Then suddenly, thankfully, Mariah took over. I glanced up. Had someone changed that deliberately?

"This is the exact opposite of fun for me," Sebastian said, bringing me back to the moment.

I stood straight and put my hands on my hips. "Sebastian Fox, it's like you've stabbed me through my garland-bedecked heart with a candy cane. You don't like Snowsly?"

"I love Snowsly," he said, making a rough attempt at fluffing the branches. I appreciated the fake effort. "It's Christmas I have a problem with."

I took a sudden step back from the tree, as if one of the wires holding the lights had given me a small electric shock. "You don't like *Christmas*?"

He shrugged as if it was entirely reasonable not to like the most wonderful time of the year. I actually half-sang the thought in my head. How could anyone not like Christmas?

I took a couple of steps closer to him and looked right at him, into his eyes. I hadn't noticed how blue they were—light, and flecked with silvery white, like he was looking at me through a snowflake. "But Snowsly *is* Christmas," I said, reaching for him and putting my hand on his jacket in an effort to pull him into the wonderful world that was Snowsly at Christmas. "We have an all-year round Christmas shop. We're known for our Christmas market. People come from miles around to drink the mulled wine from Oliver's stall. He's even bringing out his own takeaway bottle this year. And then there's the present-wrapping demonstrations. The cake stall—not to mention the tree, the decorations, the hot chocolate, and the village-wide Secret Santa."

He glanced at my hand. "The what?"

"These next couple of weeks will change your mind," I said, smoothing my hand down his lapel and then jerking my hand away. What was I doing, stroking perfect strangers? I turned back to the tree and resumed my fluffing. "You'll be pa-rum-pa-pum-pum-ing by the time the market opens in two days. I guarantee it."

"I'll be doing what?" He looked me squarely in the eye for the first time since we met. For a second it felt like the entire world had fallen away and it was just Sebastian and me decorating a Christmas tree. Just then, the opening bars of "The Little Drummer Boy" came through the speakers in reception.

What a Christmas coincidence.

"This," I said, grinning. "This song. Guaranteed ear worm and Christmas classic. You'll be humming it in no time."

If Sebastian didn't like Christmas, I was going to add him to my to-do list. He'd be right there at the top: *Convince Sebastian of the joy of Christmas.* Over the next two weeks, he'd come to see that Christmas in Snowsly was joyful and magical and a thing to be celebrated. These were the best weeks of the year for me—even if last year's festive season had culminated in the worst day of my life. Who needed to think about that? Certainly not me. Not when there was a grinch to convert in just two weeks' time.

THREE

Sebastian

What I should be doing right now was sipping whiskey in the first-class lounge at Heathrow. Instead, I was "fluffing" Christmas trees with Christmas's biggest fan. I kept telling myself that I was doing this for Granny and that I should just zone out, but it was more difficult than I expected. Maybe it was the Christmas music on a loop, or the fact that everyone was talking in hushed tones about how the Manor hadn't been fully decorated—despite the fact that everywhere I looked, shiny baubles and candy canes stared back. Maybe it was the fact that Celia was like a puppy with a new bone.

If I discounted the Christmas jumper, Celia could pass for attractive—bright blue eyes, long blond hair in a weirdly shaped plait down her back, and slim, dexterous fingers that worked at light speed on the Manor's tree. But her enthusiasm for all things Christmas meant she bordered on irritating.

"Oh yes, Sebastian. That looks fantastic," she said. I'd

only swapped the large white bauble with the medium red one as she'd asked me. "You're so tall you don't even need a ladder to reach." She paused as if deep in thought. "You think we need a bigger tree?" She took a few steps back, glancing back to the door and then past the tree to the stairs, perhaps trying to assess the perfect size for a tree in the space.

"No," I said.

She laughed. "If it was up to you, we wouldn't have a tree at all, so you don't get a say."

Peter, the avuncular owner of the White Rabbit who hadn't changed one iota in the ten years since I'd last seen him, rushed in through the front door and made a beeline for Celia. His comb-over stood on end, waving like a flag in the wind, and his cheeks were ruddy from either exertion or being out in the cold. "Celia!" he shouted, his hand in the air as if bellowing her name wouldn't catch her attention. "Celia, we have an emergency."

Celia smiled what I guessed was a permanent smile. I couldn't tell if it was an act or if she was just happy all the time. "How can I help, Peter?"

He was shaking his head. "It's Snowsville. They're coming for us." He thrust his mobile phone into her hand and I couldn't help but be intrigued. Was war about to break out? Snowsville was the village about three miles west of Snowsly. It was home to the Black Swan pub and a particularly pretty little pond at the bottom of the village, from what I remembered.

"What are you showing me, Peter?" Celia asked, her smile still firmly in place.

"That's our website. Christmas in the Cotswolds dot com."

"Yes." She started to scroll up Peter's screen. "Wait, this isn't our content." Celia's smile faltered.

"Snowsville have taken it."

At that moment, Barbara burst through the door. I'd known Barbara, or I should say, Barbara had known me, since I was born. My birthday always fell in the Easter holidays and Barbara always made my cake. "They bought the website," Barbara said. "That's what Mr. Taylor at the Black Swan said. We didn't pay the renewal fee and they bought it."

I glanced at Celia, who was clutching the reception desk like she'd just missed the last lifeboat on the Titanic. "This is going to be okay." She forced a grin. "I'm sure it's nothing serious and it can be put right. Ivy always insists on doing the website. She'll know what's happened."

The four of us filtered back into the sitting room, where Granny was reading a magazine.

"I'm not great on the website stuff," Granny said as we stood before her. "But Ethan set it up for me." I had no idea who Ethan was. "He said it was all paid up and would renew every year. Have they hacked us?"

I wasn't sure anyone was hacking anyone else in the Cotswolds, though maybe winning seasonal custom had become more cutthroat than I realized. No one even locked their doors around here. It was the kind of place that if someone dropped a pound coin, homemade signs would go up asking for the owner to come forward. "Granny, is it possible that you've changed the credit or debit card you used to pay for the domain name with?"

"Domain who?" she asked.

"The name of the website," I said. "It would renew every year on a specific card."

Granny narrowed her eyes. "I got new cards a few

months back. But still from the same bank—the numbers didn't change."

Peter groaned. "That's what's happened. Snowsville have bought it right from under our noses. The scoundrels. They've been jealous of us since 1981, when we got that huge tree put up on the village green and got more people at our carol concert. This is dirty tricks. They have to be stopped and—"

"Can I ask what the big deal is?" I interrupted. "Okay, so you've lost the website. But surely, most people come because they've come before and—"

"It says, 'The heart of Christmas in the Cotswolds is the beautiful village of Snowsville'," Celia said, her voice wobbling, the sound circling my chest as she scrolled up and down the phone screen. "Word will get out that Christmas has moved."

"Christmas hasn't moved," Peter said, his voice gruff, his hands fisted. "I've got a mind to march over to Snowsville and tell them exactly what I think of their underhand tactics."

"But Snowsly has the Christmas market," I said, finding myself trying to be reassuring. The fear and concern in everyone's eyes wasn't how I remembered Snowsly—and it wasn't how I wanted to think of this place now. "That will draw people in."

"I don't know how to tell you this," Barbara said. "But Mr. Taylor at the Black Swan also told me that Snowsville are having their own Christmas market this year."

Everyone gasped and then fell silent. It was like they'd just learned Santa wasn't real. I stepped closer to Celia, wanting to soothe her somehow. She looked so broken by the news and I had the urge to make it right. Though we'd known each other barely an hour, I'd already come to appreciate her slightly maniacal enthusiasm for Christmas. It was endearing, somehow, though the same seasonal *joie de vivre* in others made my teeth hurt.

"Nothing wrong with a little healthy competition," I said, trying to take everyone's blood pressure down a couple of points. "Snowsly has the reputation of being *the* place at Christmas. Everyone wants to come here. People won't be so quick to forget. And we can do some things to counteract the lack of a website. We can set up another one and maybe—"

"Excuse me," Celia said. She brushed past me and plonked herself down on the sofa behind us, her smile firmly in place.

I turned back to the group. "I'm sure everything will be okay. Business won't collapse overnight because of this."

"I'm such a fool," Ivy said. "It probably came through my emails. I just can't keep on top of them all. There's so many."

I knew that feeling. "This isn't your fault," I said. "And we can rectify it."

"How?" Celia asked. "That website is the first to show up if you search *Christmas holidays in the UK*, or *Christmas in the Cotswolds*. For years, it's brought in a lot of business. And now with Snowsville having a market . . . Where does that leave us?"

Celia's eyes were heavy with pleading. It was the first time the happy-go-lucky woman's mask had dropped and revealed a part of Celia I hadn't seen before. She wore a desperation to make things right that didn't make sense. I couldn't help but wonder whether, as well as her smile, her enthusiasm for Christmas covered up something. I glanced around at Granny, Barbara, and Peter. They were all looking at me as if I was going to single-handedly save Christmas.

"I've solved ten bigger issues than this before lunch on a good day. I promise we'll come up with something. For now, we need to keep focused on getting the Christmas stalls put up tomorrow and having a good night's sleep, like Celia said." I couldn't believe I was trying to reassure everyone. It wasn't like I cared whether Christmas went off without a hitch. But I did care about Granny. And the people of Snowsly, who'd showed me nothing but kindness as a child. I couldn't ignore the raw need in Celia's expression. Something told me that for some reason, she was desperate to get things right. Could Christmas be that important to anyone?

"Let me go unpack, make some calls, and see what I can do."

I might not like Christmas, but I didn't like to see anyone hopeless either. Not if there was anything I could do about it.

———

AS I SWEPT through reception on the way up to the Blue Room, I caught sight of the box of Snowsly Christmas baubles. There was no one around and without thinking, I scooped up the box and took the stairs two at a time.

Before I let myself into the room, I was on the phone to my head of IT.

"It's been hacked," Katherine said. "It's not because anything didn't get paid."

"Hacked? Are you sure?" Why on earth would Snowsville be hacking Snowsly's website? It seemed completely absurd. We were talking about Christmas shops and florists in the Cotswolds, not state secrets in MI6 head-quarters.

"Absolutely certain. And it's a good job."

"Can we do anything about it?"

Katherine sucked in a breath, which I'd learnt was never good news. "I can't. Not my area of expertise. But I have a friend, Tristan . . . They call him Merlin because he's got magic powers. He can hack them right back."

"Okay then. Problem solved."

"Only thing is, he's not cheap—"

"Whatever it takes." I might not want to have cancelled my trip to Barbados and come back to Snowsly, but I was here. And I wasn't about to let any village, no matter how pretty, hack Snowsly's website.

"I'll let you know when it's done." She hung up without another word. She'd come through. Katherine didn't make promises she couldn't keep.

I shrugged my jacket off and poured myself a glass of the red wine Mary had left me. Granny must have told her what I liked. I didn't have such expensive tastes when I was last here.

I glanced at the box of baubles I'd put on the dressing table—years of Snowsly Christmases. There must be at least forty baubles in that box. I undid my cuffs and rolled up my sleeves. I wanted to see what I'd missed. I pulled open the flaps and lifted the tissue paper that covered the first layer of decorations, the most recent commemorative decorations —all the ones I'd spent in Barbados, ignoring Christmas despite invitations from Granny to spend the festive season with her. I lifted out the tray, unsure of what I was going to find among the older baubles.

"1999" was etched onto a glass snowman with an ill-fitting top hat. I'd never forget that one. It was the

Christmas we had to call the police out because my father had left the house after a terse exchange of words. He'd drunk too much whiskey and my mother had been worried once she saw the car had gone.

Turned out he'd driven two hundred meters down the road and passed out.

2001's bauble was covered in green, glittering holly leaves—the first Christmas after my parents divorced. It was a particularly grueling Christmas because I'd stored up an unreasonable amount of hope that their separation might mean we could enjoy the holiday for once. It was the worst year I could remember. My mother had bought my father a gift but he hadn't reciprocated, and to make matters worse, he'd muttered a comment about her not "getting him" under his breath. Things escalated to a point I spent the afternoon under my bed. Neither of them noticed until it was time for my father to leave.

"2008" caught my eye, painted on a large red bauble. I picked it out of its cardboard nest. That year, I'd spent Christmas day snorkeling with Griffin on the Ningaloo reef in Western Australia. I couldn't believe I could be so fucking happy at Christmas. Each of the eighteen Christmases before that had been awful—the ones I'd been able to remember anyway, and no doubt the ones I couldn't. 2008 was the year I'd realized I had to let go of any expectations I had about the holiday and just do whatever I wanted to do.

And so I had—until this year.

This year, I was surrounded by people whose belief in Christmas magic had never been corrupted by bickering parents and drunk driving and calls to the police. Here, no one dreamed of escaping their family at the holidays. While I likely wasn't the only person in Snowsly with baggage, chances were good I was the only one without Christmas-themed china or festive pajamas.

All I could do now was stay strong in my convictions and not let the Snowsly Christmas fever throw me off course. I'd keep my expectations for the holiday as low as they ever were, thereby ensuring I wouldn't be disappointed. My version of a happy holiday didn't align with Snowsly's—but I'd be gone before anyone had the chance to figure me out.

FOUR

Celia

Fingerless gloved hands on my hips, I surveyed the scene. The Christmas hut people had arrived before the misty sun rose. They'd unloaded the unassembled huts onto the village green to begin to build our gingerbread-meets-alpine-village-style market. I'd learned my lesson from last year when I had to make decisions in the dark about where all the huts should go. Yesterday I put neon markers on the ground. It was working, and the first hut was almost up and in perfect position. The day was off with a bang.

The frigid air drew ribbons of white breath around the four workmen and I shivered, getting colder just by looking at them. Coffees distributed, it was time to get to work.

I unzipped my long, padded coat from the bottom and pulled out a hammer from my toolbelt.

"Is that a . . . Christmas-themed toolbelt under your coat?"

I looked up to find Sebastian in front of me. What was it with men who could roll out of bed and look like . . . well,

Sebastian? It just wasn't fair. Suddenly a little self-conscious of the red and white candy canes sticking out of my hat, I straightened its headband.

"Well, it doesn't fit over my coat."

"Not my point. I'm interested in the fact that you have a *specific* toolbelt for Christmas. Or maybe Christmas is a year-long obsession for you?"

"Good morning to you, Sebastian," I replied, painting on the biggest smile I could muster. I was developing a theory that Sebastian was *pretending* not to like Christmas. The way he'd taken control of the room yesterday when we were all spiraling with panic about the website was impressive and more than a little sexy. My dad always said you saw the heart of a person in times of crisis, and if that were true of yesterday, Sebastian was more complicated than he first appeared. He was grumpy, yes, but obviously cared enough about Christmas in Snowsly to help. "It's so nice of you to be up so early."

"Wouldn't want to miss this," he said, his sarcastic tone suggesting that here was the last place he wanted to be.

"You want a coffee? I have a flask and cups all set up on the trestle table. And I baked breakfast flapjacks with added cinnamon, which, if you squint, is almost healthy."

"I'm fine. What can I help with?"

"Take your pick. There are twenty-three wood huts to build. And another two to pull out of my hat."

"If any hat is going to produce German Christmas market stalls, it will be that one." He raised his eyebrows in restrained horror and I couldn't help but smile at him. There was just something so adorable about someone so grumpy.

"Thank you for giving me ho-ho-hope." I grinned at him. "Keep your fingers crossed. But before I learn magic,

I'm going around, hammering in any protruding nails with this." I held up my hammer. "And checking everything is screwed and secured properly. Then, I'm attaching lights to each stall. Again with the hammer. And hooks."

"Sounds like a lot of work. Need an assistant?" He didn't sound enthusiastic. But I appreciated that he was up at just past seven thirty, offering to help. It didn't hurt that help came in a Sebastian-shaped package. He hadn't gotten any less handsome overnight.

"Absolutely. The lights are in those crates over there."

We set to work on the first stall that had been assembled by the deliverymen. Sebastian patiently shifted loops of lights from left to right as I made sure everything was lined up. We moved onto the second stall, working faster this time, when he realized what to do. It helped that he was so tall—he didn't even need a ladder to reach the apex of the roof.

"You think anyone's going to notice if the lights aren't exactly centrally placed on each stall?" he asked after he'd moved the set of lights on the fourth stall back and forth one too many times.

"I just want it to be perfect."

"There's no such thing," he said. "Perfect would be me sitting on a beach in Barbados reading the *Economist* and sipping margaritas."

I stopped and glanced at him. He couldn't be serious about celebrating Christmas in the sun, could he? "Nice thought, but not over Christmas."

He chuckled. "*Especially* over Christmas. But instead, I'm here. Moving strings of lights left and right ten centimeters."

Maybe I'd been a bit controlling about the lights. But it looked nice if all the huts had the lights in the same place.

Lights made everything magical. They disguised flaws, made sure special festive treats weren't missed, and made people happy. They had to be right.

"You were going to Barbados? For Christmas. Are you serious?" I couldn't imagine Christmas when you didn't have to wear nineteen layers to keep your bodily organs alive, let alone Christmas in bona fide heat. "Do they celebrate over there?"

"Barely," he replied. "And I have a private beach. I see no one but the staff, I don't leave my villa, and I'm clear I don't want to hear or see anything about Christmas."

I took a step back like something he had might be catching. "You . . . cancel Christmas?"

"Right, the light is staying there. It's absolutely fine," he said, releasing the string of lights he'd been holding onto the hook we'd attached. "What's next?"

I was frozen to the spot, watching Sebastian, trying to catch a clue as to why he would deliberately avoid such a wonderful time of year. His expression was cold and unflinching, like someone being offered the cutest, tiniest puppy to snuggle with, but staying ten feet away because he'd been bitten on his arse the last time he tried to pat a dog. "I want to know why you hate Christmas so much. And I want to know why on earth you're at the center of all things Christmas in the entire British Isles, if you find the holiday so offensive."

Sebastian sighed. "Your hair is caught."

I turned and sure enough, my plait had been caught in the wires of the set of lights I had in my hands. I started to tug the top of my hair, trying to free it, when Sebastian stepped forward and stopped me. His body provided a shield from the slight breeze in the air, and I felt instantly warmer with him close.

"Hold the lights. I'll unpick you. Although I would have thought having Christmas lights attached to you on a permanent basis would be manna from heaven for you."

"So you're a business mogul *and* a comedian?" I deadpanned. "Who knew?"

He chuckled as his fingers pulled and worked my hair. He was firm but gentle, and he moved with authority like he could be relied on to free anything that was caught. Fix anything that was broken. "With a sideline in putting up fairy lights."

I faked a swoony sigh, though it wasn't much of a stretch. It was hard not to swoon with Sebastian so close. "You're a real Renaissance man, Sebastian."

"Don't forget that I also free plaits from electrical equipment." He took the armful of lights from me and stepped back, creating distance between us and opening me up to the cold breeze. I shivered. "There, you're free. How long is your hair, anyway?"

"Thanks. It comes to somewhere around my hips when it's down. It's in my family. Swedish blood."

"That explains the elfin princess look."

I clutched my chest dramatically. "Did you just give me a compliment? Is being in Snowsly thawing that ice-cold heart of yours and letting you see the magic and wonder of the season?"

A smile threatened at the corners of his mouth and he looked over to the Christmas tree, like he didn't want to look me in the eye in case it made him properly smile. "Not likely. Don't assume I meant it as a compliment."

I laughed. "Oh, I wouldn't dare. I might have known you less than a day, but I can tell compliments from a man like you aren't forthcoming in the holiday season."

He glanced at me and covered up a chuckle with a cough. "What's next?"

"Just more lights for the next five or nine hours or until your fingers fall off from not having any gloves."

We worked all day, putting up lights, checking the stalls. Sebastian returned Mrs. Bentley's dog when he came racing across the green with a mangled toy elf in his jaws. I topped up the flasks with tea and coffee and fended off tomorrow's stallholders, telling them they couldn't nab a stall early and that all places would be decided tomorrow by picking names out of a Christmas hat of my choosing.

"What's next?" Sebastian asked. He approached me at the makeshift tea and coffee station just as the sun disappeared from the horizon. The place was starting to look even more magical, with the lights twinkling against the inky sky.

"Next is learning magic. I'm no closer to a solution to finding two additional stalls."

"We're off," the stall delivery guys called over to us as they wandered back to their truck, tools, jackets, and exhausted faces accompanying them.

Those last two stalls went up really quickly. I glanced across the green at my neon markers. There were three empty spots. Three.

"Hey," I called out. "What happened to the last stall?"

The two that stopped to listen just shrugged. "We've put up everything we had in the van," one of them said.

"I was meant to have twenty-five huts," I called, walking over to the guy who seemed to be in charge. "And then they called and said there were only going to be twenty-three. And now you've put up twenty-two. I need more huts."

"Sorry, that's all we have. You can check the van if you like."

My heart sank. I pulled out my necklace, zip, zip, zipping it along its chain between my thumb and forefinger.

I wasn't sure how to find two extra huts, let alone three. What could I do? Demand the men use their own magic and rustle up additional stalls? It wasn't their fault.

"We'll figure it out," Sebastian said from behind me.

I suppose he meant to be reassuring, but his words sounded more like a platitude. *Figuring something out* was about as likely as me flying to Barbados for the day. It was just completely unrealistic.

"How?" I said, spinning around to face him. "I'm completely out of ideas. It's not like I can just set them up on tables because it's bound to be raining or snowing. Whatever they're selling needs to be protected from the elements and then on top of it all, it needs to be festive." We weren't going to figure this out. It was going to be a disaster.

He nodded like he was placating me, but I didn't want his sympathy or support. I needed help. An idea. A solution.

"Don't worry about it." He pulled out his phone and started checking messages. He held up his finger when I started to speak, then wandered off toward the tree in the middle of the green to take a call.

I sighed and turned my back. I was sure Sebastian had bigger fish to fry than the Snowsly Christmas market. Maybe I could buy some of those canvas gazebos and decorate them? It wouldn't be first choice for any of the stall-holders—it would be cold and unprotected from the elements—but perhaps three of them serving food and drink would be prepared to take them? Wasn't it always a bit too warm in the food-service huts?

"Okay," Sebastian said as he returned. "I've dealt with it. Can't get these German hut things, but I've found us something and it will work. People will be here first thing tomorrow to set up. It won't leave us much time to get them decorated, but if we all pitch in, we can do it."

Hope fluttered in my chest and I narrowed my eyes. "What have you done?"

He turned his phone to face me. "I just bought three of these."

A large, see-through igloo dome filled the screen. "They're bigger than the huts. But we've got room. Customers can go into them, or the stallholders can just serve people at the door and people can see what they want through the see-through walls."

I tipped my head to look at him. Was he for real? Had he really just solved our bordering-on-catastrophic problem with a swipe of his mobile and a phone call? Who was this man? A sorcerer? The igloos weren't exactly consistent with our theme, but if we grouped them together near the central tree, it might seem intentional. "And you say they're going to arrive . . . tomorrow?" I must have misheard him or maybe he was joking. I couldn't be this lucky, could I?

"Yes. And they will be erected by the people who deliver them. We probably need to buy some additional Christmas lights and decorations, but operation Pull Christmas Market Stalls Out of Your Hat is officially complete. I told you we'd figure it out." He made it sound like it was no big deal, but it was everything. And *we* hadn't figured it out. He had.

Sebastian might not like Christmas, but he was looking increasingly like my Christmas fairy godmother.

"You're amazing," I said, a little dumbfounded. I reached for the lapel of his coat, a second away from pushing up on my tiptoes and placing a kiss on his cheek. "Thank you."

The tops of his ears burned red, and he shrugged. "I troubleshoot. It's what I do. It's what all CEOs do. And anyway, you gave me the idea because you said you always hoped it snows on market day."

Before I could deny any of the credit, my phone buzzed. "It's Ivy," I said as I accepted the call and put it on speaker.

"Celia, dear. When you're finished, can you and Sebastian pop into the Manor? I need a word with you two."

I glanced at Sebastian, who had his hands pushed into his pockets. I couldn't tell if he was being surly or just cold. "Sure," I replied. "We'll be right there."

We crossed the village green toward the Manor in silence, Sebastian stepping ahead to open the front door and guide me in.

"Good evening, Granny." Sebastian bent to kiss Ivy on the cheek. "Can I get you anything?"

"I have an entire hotel staff at my disposal, Sebastian. You are not my nurse. Now, take a seat. Both of you."

Sebastian took one of the velvet wingback chairs next to his grandmother and I sat opposite him.

Ivy sighed. "I hate to say it, but I'm getting old. First the ankle and now the monumental fuck-up with the website."

Sebastian began to chuckle. It was the first time I'd seen him laugh since he arrived. The corners of his eyes crinkled in collusion with his mouth and the vibration of his amusement created a warmth that circled in my stomach. I couldn't help but smile, a completely genuine smile—not in response to Ivy's swearing, but because Sebastian was so diverted.

"Granny, you know you're not meant to swear in front of your grandchildren."

Ivy rolled her eyes. "I always got in trouble for that, didn't I?" She grinned, her eyes dancing in delight.

"I learned all my best swearing from you," Sebastian said. "Better than anything my parents taught me."

"Now, now, Sebastian. Let's get to the point. Because of my shitty IT skills—" This time Ivy laughed first, then Sebastian, and I couldn't help but join in. I'd never heard Ivy swear. Even when the toaster caught on fire in the Manor kitchen and the fire brigade had to be called out.

Sebastian cleared his throat. "Yes, Granny, you're banned from being in charge of anything internet related. But actually, you didn't forget to pay for the domain name. There was a technical issue."

"A technical issue?" I asked. "What does that mean?"

Sebastian shrugged. "I had one of my team look into it. So here it is." He fiddled with his phone and then handed it to me. Sure enough, the Christmas in the Cotswolds site was fully restored, with our old photographs, lists of all the shops in the village, details of the market and the present-wrapping station and the children's activities and everything.

I collapsed back in my seat.

It was a Christmas miracle.

"But how?" I asked.

"I'll tell you another time. The important thing is it's back. It's been gone about three weeks, so it may well have cost you some business, but if nothing else, you'll have it for next year." He was right—the weeks leading up to the market were when the website had the most hits, but at least we had it back for now. "But in case you run into . . . technical issues again, I think we should have other ways to find our customers. I've had an idea of how you might do that."

For someone who hated Christmas, Sebastian sure was being helpful.

"I'm presuming that each shop in the village has a mailing list of customers that have bought from them?"

Sebastian glanced from me to his grandmother.

"I have no idea," I said. "We can ask them."

"Yes, we should. If they don't have a list, they need to start collating one. Then we can get each shop to email their customers about the Christmas market."

My ribcage lifted in my chest. "That's a great idea. I should have thought of it."

I glanced at Ivy and she winked at Sebastian. "I knew you'd be great for us."

Sebastian shrugged.

Ivy turned to me. "Isn't he wonderful?"

The heat radiating off my cheeks could have melted Olaf the snowman. "It's a really great idea. These next couple of weeks can make or break some of the families of this village. Without the Christmas market, many of the shops would be forced to shut and the families that have been in this village for generations would have to move out. You being here to help us is so important." He might not be in sunny Barbados, but what he was doing here was making a difference. To the entire village. To me.

"We'll figure it out," Sebastian said—not for the first time today. I realized the phrase wasn't dismissive—it was a promise. And for just a second, it felt as if I was as light as a snowflake, without a care in the world. I believed him. I could look into those silver-flecked blue eyes and know that everything was going to be okay.

"Celia's right," Ivy said. "You're here because your Granny asked you to come and you'd do anything for me. I'm grateful for that. But you need to see that it's not just me that needs you, Sebastian. It's Celia. It's the entire village."

"I understand," Sebastian said.

"We're back on track, which is great, but we need to stay vigilant. Keep ahead of things. I'm relying on you two."

"We've got it handled," Sebastian said. "Just focus on resting and getting better."

"I'm going to be just fine," Ivy replied. "I'm all ready for hanging the annual bauble on the Snowsly Christmas tree at the opening of the market."

"Granny," Sebastian said with a growl. "You're going to be resting at the opening of the market."

"Over my dead body. Actually, that's what I wanted to talk to you about. I've hired a wheelchair so I can get to the green. Can one of you pick it up for me from Moreton tomorrow morning?"

"A wheelchair?" Sebastian asked as I tried to think how we'd get a wheelchair into my Mini. I'd have to ask Howard for a special favor, even though he'd be busy decorating his stall tomorrow.

"I don't want to hear anything about me not going out in a bloody wheelchair. It's not like I'm telling you I'm going to ice skate over to the tree. I've been putting the annual bauble on the Snowsly Christmas tree for forty years. A sprained ankle won't stop me from doing it for the forty-first year."

Sebastian sighed but didn't respond, presumably knowing Ivy better than to argue with her. His grandmother was a force no one wanted to reckon with.

"Nope," he said, suddenly. "There's no way you're going up to the green tomorrow. But there's nothing written in the rulebook that says you *have* to put the bauble on the tree *before* the market opens. Maybe it would be better to make a ceremony out of it when the market is in full swing. You'll feel a little stronger and everyone will be there to watch."

Ivy said nothing but I could almost see her brain whirring.

"Yes," I said. "A bauble ceremony might be another attraction to draw in the crowds. If not this year, then in the future. I'll have a think about what else we could add to the occasion. Maybe a brass band playing carols or—"

"You and Sebastian should put your heads together," Ivy said. "You're a great team."

Sebastian was a great team all by himself, that much was clear. All I did was hand him the problem. He solved it.

"This time next week then," Ivy mumbled.

"If you're feeling better," Sebastian said.

"This time next week," Ivy repeated. "Now, it's time for bed. Mary," she called out. "I need a hand upstairs. Sebastian, will you see Celia home, please?"

"I'm completely fine," I said. "Just across the green."

"It's dark out there. The Christmas stalls have been put up and goodness only knows what those men left behind. I don't want you tripping over something. The last thing we need is you down with a bad ankle or a broken leg or something. Sebastian doesn't mind walking you home, do you, Sebastian?"

"Be happy to," he said, his surly expression giving away what an inconvenience it was to him.

"And maybe you can come up with some good ideas about the bauble ceremony at the same time," Ivy said. "You should show him your decorations as well, Celia. Your cottage always looks so pretty. Off with you, then." She waggled her finger in our direction. Neither of us argued as we got up and left, Sebastian needlessly accompanying me across the green.

FIVE

Sebastian

Celia only lived across the green from the Manor, but within seconds of leaving the warmth of the fire in Granny's sitting room, the cold had burrowed under my clothes and started to wind itself around my bones.

"If it's this cold and clear tonight, I'm hopeful for some blue sky tomorrow," Celia said, putting a positive spin on something hopeless. I hadn't known her long but I knew that was her MO. "Hopefully that will make more people come out and see the market."

I pushed my fisted hands deeper into my pockets. I wasn't sure it ever got this cold in London. Or maybe I just didn't walk anywhere to feel it. I was always hopping from car to building. I glanced up. "You can see almost every star in the sky here." I used to lay out on the green at night for hours watching this sky. I couldn't remember the last time I'd even looked up at night. In London there was no point—there was nothing to see.

Celia laughed, her breath dancing and twirling in front

of her. It was dainty. Just like her. "Almost. When we get off the green, more will appear—the lights from the Manor and the pub completely disappear."

"You seem to have cheered up since you found out about the website," I said.

"Well of course." She shook her head as we got to the edge of the green. "It's amazing news. Thank you. And the igloos. They are genius."

I hadn't brought it up to get her thanks. It was just *this* Celia was different to the one in the meeting last night when I'd first met her. Both had wide smiles and endless enthusiasm, but tonight's Celia had a little less tension in her jaw. Her shoulders sat a little lower and she didn't look like she had a thousand thoughts in her head she was trying to sift through. Presumably the website and igloo were the reasons for her change in mood, but why? Why was Christmas in Snowsly that important to her?

"Do you always spend Christmas in the village?" I asked.

"Ever since I moved here five years ago." She stopped to reach under her coat, resuming our walk only after she'd extracted a large, black torch.

"Should I ask where that's been?" I asked.

She laughed as she switched it on. "I really need an extension on my toolbelt so it will fit over my coat."

"You use it a lot then? I can't remember when I've last done such physical work. Probably when I went and built roads in South America on my gap year."

"*You* built roads?"

"A long time ago."

"And now you're some kind of business mogul slash comedian who doesn't own gloves." She reached and pulled my arm from my pocket as if she needed evidence. Her touch was soft but determined, which seemed to sum her up. She always had a smile, but I could see that it masked a determination to get Snowsly's Christmas off the ground without a hitch. "I'm surprised you have any fingers left after today. It's been icy. I'm going to have a dig around at home and see if I can find a spare pair large enough for you."

For a second, I thought about asking whether or not she was searching for something left over from a brother or an old boyfriend, but it was none of my business. I didn't need to get to know Celia any better.

She dropped my hand. Despite not feeling the cold, I pushed it back into my pocket.

"You like to make everything right," I said.

"You're no good to me without fingers," she replied. "I'm just being practical. Anyway, you're one to talk after today. You've been like a Christmas wizard."

I'd done it for Granny. That's why I was here, after all. "So, I presume you own a shop in the village. What do you sell?"

"A shop?" Celia laughed like it was the most ludicrous thing she'd ever heard. "What made you say that? My life is far more boring than running a shop in this beautiful village. I build analytic models out of census data."

I chuckled. Of all the things I imagined Celia to be, that didn't make the top one hundred. But now she'd said it, it sort of suited her. She was clever and detail-orientated and wanted everything to be just so.

"Sometimes I wonder if I'd be better suited to floristry. Or maybe running an art gallery. In the meantime, turns out, I'm pretty good at cutting data. And don't tell anyone, but . . ." She put her forefinger over her wide smile. "I actually quite like it."

From data analyst to Christmas connoisseur. Who knew? "I assumed you were going to tell me you owned the Christmas shop."

She grinned as she nodded toward Delphinium Row. "Yes, that would be fun. I'd get to be surrounded by baubles and tinsel all year long." She paused and twisted the torch in her hand. "I don't know, though. Maybe it would take some of the magic away if I were surrounded by it all the time."

I snorted. "What magic?"

"You still haven't told me why you hate Christmas. It's so full of joy and cheer. What's not to like?"

"Is it though?" I asked. There wasn't anything joyful about my Christmases as a child. They were about as magical as an old sock.

"Of course. It's a festival of lights, a time to come together—to eat, drink, and be merry."

"It's not religious to you, then?"

"Not particularly. The human race has always needed something to cheer them up during the dark, short days of winter. The winter solstice, Christmas, Hanukkah, the birthdays of Zeus and Jupiter—actually, let's not even go down the pagan god route, because there are like fifteen of them or something who all had their birthday around this time. All I'm saying is that Juliet was right when she said, 'a rose by any other name would smell as sweet.'" She grinned as she opened a wrought-iron gate in front of a thatched cottage. "That's what my mother said to me when I asked her if Santa was real." She laughed at the memory. "I didn't have a clue what she meant but I was so confused I didn't ask again. My parents always made it so special for me as a child and I'm determined that it will be special forever. But this year, *especially* this year, Christmas has to be perfect."

"Nothing's ever perfect. Better just to accept that and get on with life. It's just a day. It will pass like all the others."

We came to a stop on her front step. Celia's white-blonde hair lit up her face. Her cheeks were flushed pink from the cold of the night and matched the tip of her nose.

"No more deflection," she said. "Why do you hate it so much?"

I shrugged, a little thrown by her insistence. But there was something about that determined streak of hers that drew me in. "Too many ruined Christmases as a child, I suppose. My parents didn't like each other. At all. And they weren't afraid to show it. Even after they divorced, they insisted that the three of us spend the festivities together, which meant Christmas was unbearable for my entire child-hood." Every year I went into each festive season with the same hope and optimism that Celia seemed to have in abundance. And every year that same hope and optimism would be extinguished little by little, by the relentless arguing of my divorced parents. Even when they weren't throwing insults and accusations at each other, the atmosphere could be cut with a Christmas cake slice. "Maybe it would have been different if I'd been allowed to come to Snowsly."

"You wanted to come?" she asked.

I nodded. I'd begged my mother every year to be allowed to come to Granny's. Partly because I always felt at home here—it was where I spent all my school holidays when I was growing up. "Of course. Christmas in Snowsly is the stuff of legends. I was desperate to experience it for myself."

Every year, my pleas to my parents were met with incredulity. They couldn't understand why on earth I didn't want to spend the festive season with them. Perhaps they thought they were better at pretending to be friends than they were. But even as a child it was patently clear they couldn't stand each other. And they didn't love me enough to fake it. Not well, anyway.

"But as you grew up and were able to choose for yourself, why didn't you come?"

It was an obvious question without an obvious answer. "I suppose I didn't want to be . . . reminded of everything I'd missed. And I was just out of hope that this time of year could be anything other than awful."

"Out of hope?" Celia reached for my lapel like she'd done earlier. Between her touch and the kindness in her expression, there was something reassuring about us being connected. Even if it was in a small way. "That's so sad."

"You don't need to feel sorry for me. Five-star service in Barbados isn't such torture."

I expected her to make a joke in return, pull out one of her Christmas puns, but instead silence passed between us for one beat and then two.

"Well, you're here *this* year." She straightened her spine and looked right at me. "This is the year you finally see what a magical time it is. You'll find your hope again."

Celia believed what had been done could be undone. I knew better. History couldn't be rewritten.

When I didn't reply, Celia tugged on my lapel. "Let yourself believe in the magic."

I covered her hand with mine, the tops of her fingers melting like ice cubes into the heat of my hand. She looked up at me, so earnest, so desperate to convince me, that I couldn't crush her optimism and tell her I'd tried. For years, I'd done everything I could to convince myself that the next Christmas would be different. But at eighteen, I'd stopped trying, and it was the best thing I'd ever done. I'd escaped.

My disappointment faded away when I'd let go of hope.

"I'm not giving up on you," she said. "It's natural that some Christmases are better than others. But this Christmas will be perfect. Just you wait. I'm going to make sure of it."

If anyone could make it happen, Celia could.

SIX

Sebastian

A piercing scream wrenched me from sleep and I sat bolt upright in bed. Had I imagined that? Or had the Manor gone and got itself haunted since I was last here?

When the sounds of slammed doors and rumbled voices carried up the stairs, I knew something serious had happened. I pulled on some clothes and sped downstairs, hoping against hope that Granny hadn't tried to put weight on that ankle and fallen.

I approached the huddle of people gathered at the reception desk. "What's happened? Is Granny okay?"

"It's the tree," Peter said, turning and revealing Celia in the sea of worried faces. "It's been pulled down. Probably by some Snowsville residents. I bet they're fuming since we got the website back."

"I can't believe someone would do something so mean. On purpose," Barbara said, shaking her head. "I've got people I considered friends in that village. Well, no more.

And if they think I'm going to still visit the wool show in March, they've got another thing coming."

Tempers were clearly frayed. Maybe it was the time of morning that had heightened everyone's emotions, or maybe the villagers of Snowsville really had scuttled across the hill in the dead of night and dismantled the tree. It could be payback for me getting the website back, but I still found it hard to believe that Snowsville would want to succeed at Snowsly's expense.

"We don't know it was sabotage. It could have been the wind," Celia said, her voice a little shaky. I had to fight an urge to reach for her—steady her, like she had me last night.

"Wind, my arse," Peter continued, his hair sticking out on end. "Someone's lifted the trunk of that tree out of the fixings—how is anyone's guess. Who's got access to the Manor CCTV? They might have caught the culprit."

"I've already checked. The CCTV doesn't cover it," Barbara said.

"Shall we focus on trying to get the tree back up?" I suggested. Now I was up, I might as well get busy. Besides, it might help Celia's mood if we tried to right things.

Celia had lost the positivity and determination I'd seen since I'd met her. She looked fragile. Almost broken. "We needed a crane to get it up and in place the first time," she explained. "There's no way we can get one at this short notice this time of the year. We're going to have to do without the tree."

"Where will we hang the annual Snowsly bauble?" Peter asked, as if the idea of going without a Christmas tree in the village was as ludicrous as wearing a dead fish on his head.

Celia's mouth drew into a tight line. "I have no idea anymore."

Discomfort lodged in my throat and I tried to swallow it down. I hadn't known Celia long, but it was long enough to know the despair in her voice was out of character. There was bound to be a solution.

"Celia," I said, pulling her round so she was facing me. I dipped down so she had to meet my eyes. "Now listen to me." I checked my watch. It was just approaching six o'clock. Sweet baby Jesus, I'd forgotten how early this village liked to be up in the mornings. "We have an army of Snowsly residents to help and we are going to figure this out. You need to be sure of it. Then the rest of us can be sure of it. Everyone's looking to you. You need to know that Snowsly is going to have the most successful, most joyous, most Christmassy Christmas of all time."

She lifted her head and looked at me as if I might be able to help. This Christmas stuff was more important to her than just making sure the shopkeepers had an opportunity to meet their revenue targets. It was clearly deeply personal. I just didn't know why. "You really think it's possible?"

"I know it is. And so do you."

She nodded her head. "I suppose. Worst-case scenario, we could always put the bauble on one of the beech trees around the green this year."

"I like that idea," Barbara said. "After all, they all have lights on as well."

"It would be a good second option," Celia said, her eyes brightening. She seemed to uncurl herself, brushing off the signs of despair. "Let's see if Sebastian is right and we can, by some Christmas miracle, get the tree back into position."

"That, I fear, is hopeless," Peter replied. "We'd need a crane, and the trunk has split at the bottom."

"Let's survey the damage," I said, not wanting Celia's mood to sink back into the ground.

The four of us filed out, strode across to the center of the green, and arranged ourselves around the fallen tree. It was difficult to see how the tree had come out of the sunken metal holder that, by all accounts, had been specially made and buried deep in the ground.

"See," Peter said. "The base is all misshapen. We can never fit it back in there, even if we could find a crane."

Celia was studying the trunk. "We can saw the end off of it. Get rid of the split bit of the trunk."

"But how will we get it back up?" Barbara asked, looking to Celia.

"I don't know anyone with a crane," Celia said. "But what if we attached a rope to Fred's tractor and tried to pull it up and slide it into place? If we had enough people helping—guiding it and steadying it while it was being lifted—it might work."

"Could work," I said. I liked her creativity. She'd gone from hopeless to determined in just a few minutes, and now had a plan A and a plan B. I could use her back in the office. If half my staff were as creative and determined as Celia, we'd be smashing our targets and I'd be spending longer than Christmas in Barbados.

"It will work," Celia nodded, her usual smile unfurling on her face. "Yes." She pulled out her phone and started talking to someone—presumably Fred—about a tractor. "Right," she said, stuffing the phone back into her pocket. "We need as many people on the green as possible by eight thirty. Fred is going to help."

"What about ropes?" I asked.

"I've got some rope back in the garage," Peter said. "I'll need a hand with it though. It weighs a ton."

"I'll bring my wheelbarrow," Celia said.

"I can do that," I replied. If anyone back in London could see me here in Snowsly, they wouldn't believe it. I'd gotten used to life in a penthouse, where I never felt the cold or saw the stars, and certainly never came across a wheelbarrow from one year's end to the next. And now I was getting ready to resurrect a Christmas tree. I'd deny it if asked, but I might actually be enjoying myself a little more than I'd expected. That was the benefit of having exceedingly low expectations. I'd looked forward to being back in Snowsly over Christmas the same way I'd look forward to a root canal. It was a low bar.

Two hours, a tractor, thirty-five meters of rope and thirty residents of Snowsly later, the Snowsly Christmas tree slid back into place.

The frozen ground vibrated with jubilation. Celia turned to me and wrapped her arms around my waist. "We did it."

I patted her on the back, partly taken aback by her show of affection and partly because her arms felt a little too good. "*You* did it."

"Thank you for believing in me."

"You're more than capable of removing any obstacle in your way. I'm sure you'll get your wish and make this the most perfect Christmas ever."

She grinned. "Anything's got to be better than last year." She spun and pulled Peter into a hug before I could ask her to elaborate.

Anything's got to be better than last year? I wanted to pull her back and get her to tell me what had happened. But she was already off, smiling and hugging and cheering with her neighbors and friends.

As victorious as Celia was in this moment, I couldn't

ignore the glimmer of sadness—or was it resignation?—I'd noticed in her eyes every time she talked about last Christmas. What exactly had happened? And how could I get someone so determined to put the past behind her to drag it all back into the present?

SEVEN

Celia

Today had started off disastrously, yet now, I felt close to invincible. The market stalls were ready and looking fantastic, thanks to Sebastian. We'd gotten the website back, thanks to Sebastian. And the Christmas tree was up and even more magnificent than it had been since it was toppled, if that was even possible. Sebastian had guided the trunk into position with the force of ten men. The suit he'd sported on the first day suggested power and control, but it had camouflaged his brute strength. I'd had to remind myself to focus on the direction of the trunk several times as my gaze slid to Sebastian's thick, sinewy forearms, and I felt his grunts of exertion between my legs.

Once the trunk was in place, we'd even managed to secure the tree with some guide ropes. If it had been the wind last night that had lifted it out of the ground, it wouldn't happen again.

Christmas in Snowsly was back on track to perfection.

"It sounds like you all had a very productive day," Ivy

said, bringing to an end the daily Christmas committee meeting.

"The entire village did," I replied. "Everyone joined in."

"I thought we all deserved a little tipple," Mary interrupted as she came into Ivy's living room, pushing a drinks trolley set with six glasses and a punchbowl. "Don't tell Oliver, but I've whisked up some of my own mulled wine recipe."

"What a wonderful idea," Ivy said. "I'm not sure why I didn't think of it myself. We certainly have a lot to celebrate."

"We still have to hope that the loss of the website hasn't hurt us too badly," I replied. "But we're in the best possible place to try to beat last year's first day sales at the market." I took the glass of mulled wine from Mary, sinking in to its warmth. I chinked my glass to Barbara's before taking a soothing sip.

"And we've even got a tree to hang the annual Snowsly bauble on when Ivy's feeling up to it," Peter said. "If it hadn't been for you two, Celia and Sebastian, I'm not sure we'd still be having a Christmas market in Snowsly this year."

"Cheers!" Ivy raised her glass of mulled wine. "To Celia and Sebastian."

"We all played our part," I replied. Truth be told, I'd been close to losing it when the tree came down. If it hadn't been for Sebastian pulling me to one side and knocking me off my panic spiral, I might have given up and gone home to bed.

My second sip of spiced wine made my body feel like it had been coated in a condensed, soporific syrup that slowed my senses and smothered my adrenaline. I was instantly cosy and comfortable. And entirely exhausted.

For the next half an hour, I nodded and smiled as the rest of the group continued their chatter and excitement about the day past and the market to come. I stayed silent, unable to muster the energy to speak. A couple of times I glanced over at Sebastian, who wasn't saying much either. After a fraught and physical day, he still looked yacht-party ready. His gray cashmere jumper hadn't taken a beating from being caught on the Christmas tree trunk like poor Peter's Christmas pudding jumper, which now had a huge hole just over the sprig of holly. And Sebastian's hair still had that same glossy sheen it always seemed to have. I could tell by the way my plait had started to unwind itself that I looked like a place a hedgehog would happily hibernate. I was also sporting a now-dried patch of mud up the side of my coat that I'd have to try to brush off when I got home. It looked like Sebastian had been on the sidelines while the rest of us had been at war. But that couldn't be further from the truth. Sebastian might claim to hate Christmas, but his actions proclaimed loud and clear that he loved Snowsly and his granny, and would do anything for either.

A second before I excused myself—confident that leaving would be the only way to avoid falling asleep where I sat—Ivy cleared her throat. "These old bones need to get to bed. Off with you all. Another busy day awaits. Sebastian, please make sure you see Celia home."

I started to shake my head but stopped as I locked eyes with Sebastian, who nodded.

"I'll see you home," Sebastian said as he approached me. There was something in his smooth, sultry voice I hadn't heard before. He was probably as exhausted as I was.

I didn't argue and we said our goodbyes. I pulled on my hat, coat, and gloves and headed to the lobby.

"I'll be fine. I have my torch," I said to Sebastian as we

headed to the exit. I'd left my tool belt at home this morning but carried my trusty torch at all times.

"It will only take a few minutes. Let me, please."

I sighed, too tired to argue. "Okay."

"It's icy," he said as we stepped out of the Manor.

Without thinking, I slipped my arm through his and he pulled it close to his chest, like he was hanging on to something precious. Even though the pavements were slippery, I had no doubt the man beside me would catch me if I were to fall. A pang of regret chased around my ribs as I realized I'd never felt that before. Not even with Carl.

"Thank you for the pep talk this morning," I said. "It made all the difference."

"What are friends for?" Sebastian kept his eyes on the path in front of us. "I knew you were just having a moment. You soon snapped out of it and got back to business."

Warmth gathered in my stomach and I bit down on my bottom lip. He'd had faith in me. That felt good. "Thanks to you."

"Hardly. But if I was any kind of assistance at all, it was my pleasure."

Sebastian seemed more relaxed and at home than he had done when he'd joined the meeting just a few days ago. "You seem less grumpy than you were when you arrived. Has the Snowsly ambience gotten to you?"

He chuckled as he led me toward my cottage. "Maybe I've just accepted the idea that I'm going to have to wait until the twenty-fourth to go to Barbados. It's not that far away."

"You're leaving on Christmas Eve?" My stomach flipped, disappointed for him—and maybe for me, too. What was the point in all the build-up and anticipation if he left before the big day?

"The market will be over. The Christmas committee disbanded. Granny won't need me here."

My stomach tugged at his words. As we reached my front door step, I turned to him. "She might not *need* you here, but I have no doubt that she'd love to spend Christmas with you."

He pulled in a breath as he turned to face me. "She's the center of this village. She won't even notice I'm gone."

But I would.

"You'll be missed," I said, pressing my glove-covered hands to his chest.

He glanced up at the mistletoe hanging above us, pulled his hands from his pockets, and cupped my face. When I dared to look up at him, his blue eyes seemed to burn brighter than normal.

"You should go in," he murmured, his tone pure, liquid chocolate. If I could bottle his voice and sell it to drink, we'd guarantee Snowsly was the king of Cotswolds Christmas. "It's cold."

I nodded but stayed rooted to the step. In the next moment, he leaned in and pressed his gloriously full lips against mine, soft and firm. The heat from his mouth seeped into me, warming me from the outside-in. My entire body began to vibrate.

If that's what his lips could do . . .

He pulled back and my hand flew to my mouth.

"Did I overstep?" he asked, his eyes narrowing.

I shook my head. "Never," I managed to breathe out.

The corners of his mouth turned up and he nodded. "Good night, Celia Sommers."

I watched as he strode back up Delphinium Row and disappeared into the darkness, taking with him his strong hands, half smile, and completely kissable lips.

EIGHT

Celia

My heart still fluttering like I had a butterfly trapped in my chest, I unwound my scarf from my neck and hung it on one of the hooks in the hallway.

Sebastian just kissed me.

I pressed my fingers to my lips again. It felt good. Strange to be kissed by someone who I'd only known a few days. Someone who wasn't . . . him. Even though Carl had been gone almost a year to the day, it still felt oddly disloyal.

My phone buzzed in my hand and I pressed accept on the call from my oldest friend.

"Are you awake?" she asked.

"I'm answering the phone. Of course I'm awake. It's just gone nine."

"I thought it was eleven."

"Lemon, you've lived in New York nine years. All you need to do is add five to whatever time it is there."

"You know math was never my strong point."

"Maths. Don't forget where you come from. We call it

maths with an 's' in the motherland."

"You're in a feisty mood."

I grinned. Was I? Was that what Sebastian's kiss had done to me? "Just had a busy day. How is December in New York?" I wound my way to the back of the cottage to the kitchen and flicked on the kettle. A nice cup of hot chocolate was just what the doctor ordered.

"I wish you were here," she said.

Every year we talked about spending Christmas together, but she was paying a ridiculously high rent to live in New York and couldn't afford to come over here. Until this year, I couldn't think about spending the season in New York. Carl had his job and family and would never have wanted to be out of the country at Christmas. This year, without Carl, I was paying double the bills, so we still couldn't make it work.

And this year, Snowsly needed me.

Or maybe I needed Snowsly.

"I wish *you* were here," I said, pouring the hot water into my mug and scooping it up. As soon as I'd finished talking to Lemon, I'd head upstairs. It was early, but on these dark winter nights I liked to be snuggled up in bed with a book as soon as I came home.

"Next year," she said. "I promise, I'm coming to Snowsly next year. I'm putting aside a little every month."

"You'd love it so much." I set my hot chocolate down on the two turtledoves coaster, which was one of twelve on my kitchen table, and switched on the lights of the Christmas tree that sat on the countertop. Even if I was only here for ten minutes, it wouldn't hurt to feel as Christmassy as possible.

"Christmas in New York is pretty nice as well."

"But I'm not there, so how good can it be?" I asked,

fiddling with the angel on the top of the tree that always seemed to look as if she'd had one too many gins.

Lemon laughed. "True. It's just I'd love you to come and see it for yourself."

I collapsed into my favorite yellow kitchen chair. I'd done the calculation about seventeen times since Carl left. There was just no way I could afford to go to New York for Christmas. Although I loved Christmas in Snowsly, I'd have happily skipped it this year to get away from the memories of last year. But if I couldn't escape, I was going to make it as good as it possibly could be. A kiss from Sebastian definitely didn't hurt.

"So how's it going there?" Lemon asked. "Any more disasters?"

"It depends how you categorize me getting kissed under the mistletoe."

Lemon shrieked. "Someone kissed you? Who? Please tell me it wasn't Howard?"

I laughed at the idea that I'd be kissing a married man who was at least double my age. "You know I told you about Ivy's grandson coming up to help?"

"Is that even legal? Isn't he like, fourteen or something?"

"Yeah, no. He's not fourteen." Everything about Sebastian was grown up.

I switched to speaker and reached for the laundry basket of clean washing on the blue chair next to me that was waiting for me to take it upstairs and put it away. I started to change. I wanted to spend as much time as possible in the adorable reindeer pajamas I'd found online. The antlers were furry and one of them had a red nose that squeaked if you pressed it.

"It's happening," she said. "You're moving on."

I glanced over at the bin bag of Carl's things that I still

hadn't thrown out. He'd taken a couple of suitcases and told me he didn't want anything else. He'd left gifts I'd given him. Books he'd read, clothes, toiletries. He'd even left his Star Wars duvet cover. It was like he wanted to be purged of any memories of our relationship. I'd gathered his things and tossed them into a bag, expecting to put them out for the bin men that week. But somehow I couldn't bring myself to do it. As much as Carl wanted to purge me from his life, I wasn't ready to bleach out the memories of him.

"I'm not sure I'm moving on, but Carl isn't the last man to have kissed me." It was a relief, but painful at the same time.

"So, has this Sebastian thing got legs?"

"*He's* got legs." Long ones. Lean, muscular, lovely legs. Or so I imagined. "But he and I don't have legs. He's some sophisticated businessman from London—"

"That doesn't mean—"

"Who hates Christmas."

I could have heard Lemon's sigh across the Atlantic even if she hadn't been on the phone. "That's a problem."

I laughed. "It is. But I don't need him to be *the one*. It just feels . . . like a part of me has woken up."

"About time. Have you gotten rid of that nasty Star Wars duvet cover yet?"

I'd hated Carl's duvet cover for so long. We'd had numerous rows about it. No grown man should have an image of Darth Vader on his pillow. The argument would always take a swift turn to the "Christmas invasion," as he called my love of seasonal decoration. And I always ended up relenting.

"Not yet," I confessed.

"Celia, don't you think it's telling that it was Darth Vader and not Yoda or Luke that he had on his pillow?"

I laughed. "Carl wasn't evil."

"Wasn't he? He left you on *Christmas Eve*. Only the worst kind of person does something like that, let alone to someone who loves Christmas as much as you do."

"I don't want to talk about it." The buzz of excitement that had been with me since Sebastian's kiss was swept away by the memories of this time last year. Carl had said he'd wanted to be in charge of dinner on Christmas Eve. I had an inkling that he might be up to something that involved my left ring finger. He'd checked about one hundred and twenty-two times that I hadn't signed up to man the decoration-making station at the market on Christmas Eve. Then when Lemon told me he'd asked about my ring size, I'd been completely certain we were going to get engaged—at my favorite time of year no less. It was going to make Christmas even more special to me than it had been before.

And then rather than ask me to marry him, he announced he was leaving me.

Since then, it was as if I'd spent nearly an entire year waiting for him to reappear and decide he wanted his things and our relationship back. I couldn't bring myself to part with his stuff—even the stuff I'd hated when we were together. Part of me had been holding out hope that he'd come back as abruptly as he'd left and want our lives together to go back to the way they'd been before. It would be like he'd never been gone at all.

But he *was* gone.

He'd been gone a long time, and he wasn't ever coming back.

But Sebastian was here. He was here, and he had kissed me, and I'd bet good money he didn't sleep under a Star Wars duvet.

NINE

Sebastian

I never expected the Snowsly Christmas market to be so busy. Cars were almost parked on top of each other all around the village, hordes of people were gathered around the hot chocolate stand, and a coach full of tourists had just pulled up. No wonder this village did most of its business in these few weeks.

The small, subdued lights threaded through the branches of the beech trees that circled the green and then the more dazzling lights of the Christmas tree in the middle offset the gray sky overhead. The cold wind that was so biting when I'd gone around the back of the Manor to take out some rubbish, seemed to skip over the green completely. Maybe it was the chestnuts roasting on the far side, or the pumpkin and ginger soup in crunchy sourdough bread bowls being sold at the bakery's stall. Whatever it was, the air carried a delicious scent and everyone was so damn happy. Even the Christmas music playing from discreetly positioned speakers didn't dent my mood.

As I walked up the high street, I could see it wasn't just the stalls that were overrun with customers—the shops themselves were teeming with people. Not just the Christmas shop, but the bakery selling Christmas cakes and puddings and gingerbread; the sweetshop, which I couldn't believe had survived the decade since I was last here, had a queue out the door; and even the art gallery couldn't fit anyone else inside. Granny's call to me and Celia's stress about things going wrong had been well-founded. If not for the Christmas custom, I wasn't sure how some of these businesses would make it through the rest of the year.

This amount of tourism couldn't be taken for granted, and people having this much of a good time shouldn't be denied.

It was the Christmas I'd dreamed about having since I was a child. I'd have had so many happy memories if I'd been here rather than at home with my parents. Resentment mixed with regret in my gut. All children should have a Snowsly Christmas.

For the first time since I arrived, I felt like an outsider. An interloper who'd trespassed into other people's joy because I'd never seen the market before. I didn't have a history of Christmases in Snowsly.

Michael Bublé finally gave way to the jingling bells of Wham's "Last Christmas," and then just as George Michael was about to burst into song, the track jumped to Kirsty MacColl and the Pogues. Hadn't that happened in the hotel yesterday as well? Maybe someone hated Wham!

I stood on the edge of the green, watching, debating whether or not I should disappear up to my room and fake a stomach bug when Celia stepped out of the herd of people around the stalls and started toward me. I tamped down the flicker of the smile that threatened at the edges of my mouth. I hadn't planned on kissing Celia last night, but I couldn't regret it. She'd tasted of red wine and oranges, and she'd been as warm as the roaring fire in the Manor's reception.

"Your market is a triumph," I said as she beamed at me.

"The *Snowsly* market is going quite well. It doesn't belong to anyone. Certainly not me. The loss of the website hasn't been completely catastrophic. Thanks to you." She glanced down at the paper I was clutching. "What's that?"

"Peter's mailing list. He only has a hard copy. I've said I'll get it transferred to an electronic format. And I've had my marketing department work up some graphics and wording for the market. The idea is each business can use the same templates when they mail their customers about coming to visit Snowsly in the next week or so."

"That's incredible, Sebastian. Thank you."

"I made a couple of calls. It's nothing."

"I think you might be getting in the festive spirit." She smoothed her hand down the front of my jacket. Every time she was near, the air seemed warmer, the stars seemed to shine a little brighter, and I stopped hating Christmas quite so much.

"It's just business. I came to help. That's all it is."

"Well as long as you're here, you've had your name put down for Secret Santa. I have the envelope." She handed me a manila envelope. "Don't open it yet because I'm likely to wrestle you to the ground just to find out who you got."

I raised my eyebrows. "Doesn't sound like too much of a disincentive." I was pretty sure I could take Celia in any kind of wrestling match, but I wouldn't mind her *trying* to take me on. The more time I spent with her, the more I liked her. I liked her passion and energy—even if it was aimed at Christmas. I liked her creativity and determina-

tion. And I'd enjoyed our kiss. It had been just as I'd imagined—innocent, but with a hint of spice underlying her
sweetness.

She blushed under my gaze and pushed the envelope
into my hand. "I'm serious, bury it in your pocket or I'm
coming for you."

"And what if I don't want to play Secret Santa?" I
always refused to participate in the one they held in the
office.

"You have to!" she said. "We exchange gifts on
Christmas Eve, so you don't even have the excuse that
you're not going to be here."

I liked the way the idea of something as inane as Secret
Santa made her so happy, but I didn't know enough about
anyone in the village to be able to buy them a gift.

"No one except Ivy knows who's buying gifts for who.
It's a complete surprise every year. And there's a maximum
budget of twenty pounds. The only other rule is that whatever you buy or make, it's not allowed to come from
Snowsly—otherwise everyone ends up getting the same
thing. Come on. Why wouldn't you want to participate?"

The fact that I didn't have to spend more than twenty
pounds wasn't going to sway me either way. I just never
bought gifts for anyone. Not since that Christmas on the
deserted beach in Western Australia.

"Please," she said. "For me." Her eyelashes flickered
around her pale blue eyes as she looked up at me. If we
hadn't been surrounded by hundreds of people, I would
have pulled her in for another kiss. Instead, I huffed and
pushed the envelope into my pocket. Defeated.

She knew me well enough not to crow. She just grinned
at me, her face lit up at the thought that this grinch might be
growing a heart. But she had the wrong end of the stick. I

just wanted to avoid another conversation where she tried to convince me that Christmas was a magical time.

"Come on," she said, linking her arm through mine in the unselfconscious way she did. "Let me show you around. You have to have a mug of Howard's hot chocolate. I swear it's just molten chocolate, double cream and sugar."

"My arteries can't wait," I said as we strode toward the green. "The tree held up then," I said as we joined the queue at Howard's stand.

"Yes, thank goodness. Either the ropes kept the wind from lifting it or the saboteurs didn't want to risk another attack. Probably thought that now that we were on notice, we'd have people watching out, or figured we'd put some of the Manor CCTV on the tree—which we totally did."

The idea of one village tearing down another's tree seemed completely ludicrous. But Katherine had been clear —Snowsly's website had been hacked. I'd not told anyone because I didn't want to stir further anger and resentment, and no doubt it would encourage conspiracy stories about Snowsville when we needed to focus on Snowsly. "I don't think it was sabotage."

"You can't rule anything out. There's a lot of money changing hands here today. And for the next twelve days. Money makes people stupid."

She wasn't wrong about that. "Surely they could have just sawn off the branches or something if they really wanted to cause trouble. You're remarkably cynical about the neighboring villagers considering how . . ." I didn't want to say *naïve* because it wasn't a good description of who she was. "Christmas-postive you are."

"Christmas-positive? Really? Is that what the kids are calling it these days?"

I chuckled. "You know what I mean."

"Just because I know what real life is like doesn't mean I don't want it to be better." She paused as she waved at someone across the green. "I believe in possibility and potential and the idea that magic is so often waiting in the wings but just never gets called out to sing. Christmas is a time when we should invite magic into our lives. We all need to believe."

Part of me wanted to dismiss what she was saying as some kind of school-girl Instagram post telling me that all my dreams could come true. But then another part of me was taken in by what she was saying. It wasn't just her passion—it was that she was so earnest, so serious. For a woman who dealt in facts and data for a living, she seemed to find it surprisingly easy to suspend her disbelief.

"Two of your best hot chocolates please, Howard," she said as we reached the front of the queue. "How's business?"

Howard got to work frothing the milk and pouring four different ingredients into seven different cups, stirring and shaking and then adding something from what looked like a flour duster. "It's busy. Difficult to tell at this point whether we'll be up or down. And it depends how the shop is doing."

"Oh I just passed it. Full to bursting," I said.

Howard grinned as he topped cups with marshmallows. It was like watching someone at a top London bar mix a cocktail, or a magician perform a trick with flawless execution. "There you go."

Celia and I had a brief tussle about who was going to pay, but I won. We took our drinks and continued our circuit around the stalls.

"You know, he should be on a stage making those drinks," I said. "It was like theatre."

"That's not a bad idea. Maybe we could combine it with the decorations workshop."

I took a sip from my reusable mug and swallowed. "Wow, that's *really* good. But *really* bad for me."

Celia laughed. "This is why Christmas should only be once a year."

We came to Jim's stall, which wasn't at all what I'd been expecting. I wasn't sure how a florist was going to make money at a Christmas market, but the stall was full of door wreaths made of fir and pinecones, cinnamon sticks, and brightly colored baubles. How long would it take for the fir to fade?

"How's business?" Celia asked.

Jim bobbed his head noncommittally. "Busy. Not sure I'm as busy as last year. I'll submit takings numbers by midnight."

We said our goodbyes and headed on, though Celia fell quiet.

"I remember even when I was a child, Jim always expected the worst to happen," I said. "He clearly hasn't changed. Wait until you see the data before you get disappointed."

Celia nudged me. "How did you know the exact right thing to say?"

"Because I know you want Snowsly to have the perfect Christmas and it would worry you if you thought first night of the market takings were down on last year. It's why you're asking people when you know they don't know anything for sure until the market closes. But you're going to have to be patient and just wait for everyone to submit their numbers. Don't borrow trouble."

Celia nodded and linked her arm through mine again

and I tried not to enjoy it too much. We headed toward the raffle.

"So what happens on the twenty-sixth?" I asked. "Do you morph into a cynical data analyst who doesn't leave her home and barks at any villagers she sees, warning them to keep their distance?"

She stopped and laughed as if she couldn't possibly combine walking at the same time. "It's far worse. Well, the twenty-sixth is Boxing Day, so obviously that's still technically Christmas, but on the twenty-seventh I spend the day taking down my decorations."

I'd been joking, but her response surprised me. "You do? But don't you want Christmas to last forever?"

"No, I'm happy to be festive in the weeks leading up to Christmas, and the holiday itself of course. But I need contrast. I like the fresh start of a new year. Everything in the previous year is forgotten and I get to start over again, no mistakes. So even if Christmas didn't live up to expectations, it's all in the past when the New Year arrives."

"I can't imagine any Christmas would fail to live up to your expectations. You're so particular about everything. Isn't every Christmas you have perfect?" I knew something had happened last year that had upset her, and I wanted to know what. I found myself wanting to know her better.

"Far from it." She sighed. "Some things are out of even my controlling, overbearing hands."

I laughed. I couldn't have put it better myself.

An alarm sounded and Celia dug her phone from her pocket. I noticed that her Christmas tool belt had been left behind today. "It's my time to run the decoration-making station. I'd ask you to help but the children don't need to meet a real live grinch." She laughed and inexplicably twirled in a complete circle before heading off in the direction of two large tables covered in glitter and ribbons.

As she walked up to take over from Barbara, the children's faces lit up. They clearly knew her—probably from last year. And their Christmas was made all the more magical for Celia being a part of it.

All but once since I'd met her, Celia had worn a smile front and center, but more and more frequently, I hadn't been convinced that her expression reflected how she felt on the inside. This afternoon wasn't one of those times. Her grin lit up her entire face, and her white-blonde hair became almost iridescent under the lights that had been strung above the tables. I could hear her infectious laugh from here. She looked entirely at ease making a gaggle of children happy.

There was something about being in Celia's orbit that made me want to believe that good things happened to good people. That magic could be real. And that Christmas could be everything I'd ever hoped for as a boy.

TEN

Celia

I didn't let my gaze drop from Barbara's face from the moment she came into Ivy's sitting room and took a seat on the upholstered bench by the fire. She was the only one in the village who knew how all the businesses in the village had done yesterday, and she wasn't giving anything away. She didn't wear a grin, like we'd all won the lottery, but she wasn't hang-dogged and miserable either. I'd texted her last night to try to find out whether or not it was good or bad news from the first day of the market. She'd insisted she hadn't added up all the numbers. How long did it take, for goodness' sake?

For years I'd tried to convince Ivy to let me collate the numbers each day, but she'd told me that Barbara had always done it, enjoyed doing it, and that she wasn't going to be responsible for my blood pressure readings if she handed the job to me.

I was just invested, that's all. For the good of Snowsly.

I glanced around the room at Barbara, Ivy, Howard, Jim,

and Keely, trying to gauge whether or not everyone was as desperate as I was. Finally, I glanced at Sebastian. He looked as nonchalant and confident as he always did. I must ask him how he always seemed so self-possessed. "So?" I blurted, unable to hold in my anticipation any longer.

"Barbara, ignore her," Ivy said. "We shall have some pleasantries first. Did everyone enjoy themselves yesterday? Did I miss anything? How is the tree holding up?"

I took a deep breath. I swear, Ivy knew she was torturing me and just didn't care.

People chit-chatted and strung things out for as long as humanly possible. I zip, zip, zipped my pendant on its chain and bit my tongue to keep silent. Finally, Ivy said, "Barbara, tell us how we did."

Barbara took a deep breath and it was all I could do not to push her off the bench and grab the papers from her hand so I could see for myself. "It's not great."

My stomach crashed to the floor.

It must have been the impact of the website. And the rival market at Snowsville.

I'd tried so hard to make this Christmas perfect and it seemed like the harder I tried, the worse things got. I should have pushed harder to get the other villagers to accept the Ferris Wheel—that would have drawn people in. But maybe not, if Snowsville was taking all our customers. I pushed my hands through my hair and flopped back in my seat.

"We're twenty percent down on the first day compared to last year. Last year was fairly typical."

That wasn't *not great*. That was terrible.

Ivy nodded. "Well, we couldn't have done any more. We've put on a great show by all accounts."

"I'm surprised we're down," Sebastian said. The fact that he'd said "we" rather than "you" lifted my spirits. Just a little. "It was so busy. And not just the stalls. The shops as well. There were queues outside some of them. There wasn't even a spare table in the pub. I checked."

"Maybe people are visiting but aren't spending," I suggested.

"We don't measure footfall," Barbara said. "But Sebastian's right. It was busy. I wouldn't have said we were down on last year by looking at the number of people visiting."

"I have more news," Barbara said and cleared her throat. "From Mr. Taylor at the Black Swan." Her tone was somber and I just knew he was going to tell us how Snowsville had killed it yesterday. I bet that's why people weren't spending as much with us—they were taking their money to Snowsville.

"Snowsville sent people to our market last night." She glanced around as if she was getting ready to run if we started throwing things at her. "To see what we were doing. Check how busy we were. That kind of thing."

"To steal all our great ideas, you mean?" I bit out.

Sebastian squeezed my shoulder, trying to reassure me, but nothing would help. "That's not so surprising, is it?" he asked. "It makes sense for them to check out the village that's been running Christmas for years. Especially when they're so close. You're not going to stop that happening. Look on the bright side—it will push Snowsly to continue to set the bar and do better every year." His expression was all confident authority, but he couldn't convince me.

Snowsville was going to sink us.

"But we're not doing better every year," I said. "We're twenty percent down on last year."

"We need a two-pronged approach," Sebastian continued. "First, we need fresh ideas that will bring people to Snowsly to spend money, not just visit. And then we need to increase the numbers of people who are coming to the area. I have some ideas. And I can make a few calls. Leave it with me."

"Wait," Barbara said, throwing a long, searching look at Ivy. "If Snowsville knows what we're putting on for visitors, isn't it only fair that we know what they're doing?" Barbara asked. "We should visit Snowsville's market."

"Great idea," Howard said.

"Excellent," Keely replied, nodding at me like I had suggested it.

I perked up. Yes, that made sense. If they were taking our business, I'd like to understand how and why.

"We don't just want to copy them," Sebastian warned.

Jim cleared his throat. "No, but it makes sense to check out the competition."

"Yes," Howard said. "We can figure out what we need to do better." Howard was grimacing like someone had told him there was a sudden and total country-wide chocolate shortage.

"Fantastic idea," Ivy said. "But of course, I can't go. I'm too recognizable. Same for all of you lifers. It makes sense if Celia and Sebastian go. A young couple is far less conspicuous than a group of old codgers from the rival town."

I wanted to go if it would help Snowsly, but realistically, I needed to stay close to the action. Also, a couple? Why did we have to pretend to be a couple? "I have to hold the fort here," I replied. "What happens if things go wrong?"

"You're only going to be out a few hours," Ivy replied, her gaze flickering toward Barbara.

"Yes, you won't need to be long," Barbara said. "Go in the evening—that way at least you're not making it too obvious. I think it's entirely fair that we check out the competition, but we don't need to be blatant about it."

I sighed. "Okay. That's fine. I'll go on my own. I don't need to be more than thirty minutes."

"You don't want to rush it," Ivy said. "You'll draw more attention to yourself. And if Sebastian goes with you, people won't place you. No one in Snowsville will recognize Sebastian all these years later."

"There's no point in upsetting anyone unnecessarily," Howard said and cleared his throat again. Was he coming down with a cold or something? "You and Sebastian should go together."

I glanced at Sebastian, who I couldn't read at all. "I'm sure it won't take long," he said. "And I can go on my own if Celia's needed here."

"No, no, no," Ivy said at the same time as Howard shook his head and Barbara chirped, "Not at all," as if she quite relished the idea of me not being around.

"You've been working so hard," Keely said. "You might even pop into the Black Swan and have dinner or something."

"What a great idea," Ivy said. "You should go and enjoy yourselves."

I felt slightly dazed, like I'd missed a part of the conversation that explained why it was so important to visit Snowsville tonight, and why it would be almost impossible for me to go without Sebastian. Everyone seemed so resolute.

"We don't have time for dinner but if you want to come, Sebastian, I'm happy to drive." The jingle in my stomach told me I didn't hate the idea of spending the evening with Sebastian, even if it was on a mission to spy on our competition.

"Sebastian?" Ivy asked.

"I'm very happy to go, Granny."

"Then that's settled. Tonight, you and Celia will go to Snowsville and figure out what they're doing and how. I suggest we meet back here and you can both debrief us."

So it was settled. Sebastian and I would spend the evening together. And I wouldn't think about him kissing me. Not for a second.

ELEVEN

Sebastian

I ducked my head to peer through the passenger seat window of the smallest car I'd ever laid eyes on. Why on earth hadn't I had Bradley leave the car? That way I wouldn't have to have Celia drive me in a toy car.

She waved and grinned at me before beckoning me in. I wasn't sure I'd fit.

I opened the door and assessed how I was going to be able to fold myself up to fit in the front seat. "How old is this car?"

"I hope you're not *Claus*-trophobic." She laughed at her own joke. "Oh I don't know. It was born sometime in the last century. You can't say it doesn't have personality."

There were a lot of things I could say about this car. "Maybe personality isn't something that's top of my list when it comes to transportation."

"Say it ain't *snow*."

I shook my head, trying not to crack a smile at how

ridiculously awful her Christmas puns were. "It's a short drive, right?"

"Just six miles."

I groaned. That could take twenty minutes in the Cotswolds. "Does the seat go back any further?"

"'Fraid not, sorry."

If it was anyone else, I'd have point blank refused to go, but I knew it would devastate Celia and I just couldn't do that to her. After shuffling awkwardly, banging my head twice, and losing my shoe, I managed to get into the car in a position that would guarantee I'd get a cramp after five minutes. "I hope I manage to get out without you having to saw off my leg or something."

Celia laughed, and a ribbon of warmth chased up my spine. As she pulled out of the space in front of the Manor, I tried to place what was different about her this evening. I'd not seen her white woolen hat before. It was less overtly Christmassy than her usual attire, with subtle blue snowflakes bordering the headband. "I can't tell where your hair stops and the hat starts."

"It's my disguise. People always notice my hair. It's so long and . . . you know, almost white, so I've put it under the hat so people don't see it and immediately know it's me."

"I'm glad I brought my moustache and bowler hat."

"Oh and I have some camo-paint. If you don't think it's too much?"

I shot her a glance to see if she was serious, but the grin she was holding in exploded across her face, giving her away.

"Is it bad that I'm a little bit excited to be pretending to be someone else for the night?" she asked. "Should we rehearse our personas? In case we get asked questions."

Her enthusiasm wasn't limited to Christmas apparently.

"I'm not sure they're going to put a bag over our heads, haul us to the nearest police station, and start interrogating us, but if it's going to distract me from the cramp crawling up the entire left side of my body, let's rehearse."

She paused at a Give Way sign and turned right. I didn't see any signs to Snowsville but no doubt she knew where she was going. "So I was thinking we're newlyweds. We're having a mini-moon in the Cotswolds because we're saving for a deposit for a house in . . . Manchester."

Newlyweds? That was an interesting choice.

"I'm not sure either of us can pull off a Mancunian accent. I know I can't."

"Sebastian!" she said, her tone chastising. "You should believe in your-*elf*." She grinned and then fell silent for a couple of beats. "You're right. Oxford, then. Then being in this neck of the woods makes sense—we're staying close to home."

"Did we get married in Oxford?" I asked, curious as to how much thought she'd put into our cover.

"Yes. A small church in my parents' village of Wheatley. Close friends and family only."

"And what is it I do for a living?"

"You're a salesman—nope, you're a civil servant. I work as a teaching assistant but I'd really like to train to be a teacher, though I'm not sure it's worth it when we want kids as soon as possible. I probably won't want to go back to work for a while afterward."

"Kids?" Newlyweds meant lots of sex and I could heartily sign up to that idea with Celia. But kids?

"We're going to aim for three but will feel blessed with just one. I'm from a family of five so—"

"Are you really?" I asked, intrigued. Having been an only child, I always wondered what it would be like to feel you had someone by your side, even when your parents let you down. I'd always had Granny but because she didn't live with us, she wasn't always around.

"Nope. A baby brother came along when I was fourteen. I'd have liked a sibling more my own age. Neil was only four when I left for university. We've never really done that thing where you make forts under the dining room table, lie for each other, or plan to run away to escape the parents from hell. You know what I mean?"

Better than she could imagine.

"But you and I want three kids," she continued and I laughed. "We love the idea of a house filled with noise at any point of the day."

I couldn't think of anything worse, but this was just pretend so I was prepared to play along. "Are we actively trying to get pregnant at the moment. Like, should we practice?"

Her eyes went wide and a pink bloom crept up her cheeks. "I'm not sure anyone would need to know about our sex life."

I chuckled, enjoying the thought that she might be thinking what it might be like. "Where did we meet?" I asked.

"I was working a second job in a coffee bar and you were a regular customer who'd come in every lunchtime. Obviously, I had a crush on you."

"Obviously?"

She shrugged and her cheeks burned red and I couldn't help but enjoy it.

"Did I *obviously* have a crush on you too?"

She tried to bite back a smile. "Not at first. I was just some girl behind the counter taking your coffee order. But I started writing you jokes and poems on your cup. It got your attention."

I couldn't help but smile. "I was obviously won over by your excellent puns."

"Exactly!"

I was amused by her certainty. "Did I ask you out?"

She pushed her lips into a circle. "Would pretend-you have asked me out? You're a civil servant . . . A man who doesn't notice . . . Nope, you didn't ask me. One time you came in, I was at one of the tables. You sat down next to me. We got talking—our first date was almost accidental. And then you asked me."

Pretend-me didn't sound a lot like the real me. I did little by accident and if I wanted something, I wasn't afraid to ask. "I'm not sure I like pretend-me."

"You're sweet." She glanced at me, wearing a you-can't-hate-the-elaborate-cover-I-came-up-with expression.

"I'm not sweet. I hate Christmas, remember?"

"Yes, but this isn't real-you. It's pretend-you. Pretend-you is . . . Pretend-you *loves* Christmas. We should have bought matching Christmas jumpers. That would have been *snow* fun."

We had very different definitions of what "fun" involved, and I couldn't help but wonder if pretend-me was someone Celia was more interested in than real-me.

"Pretend-you sounds a lot like real-you. Am I the man you invented for yourself?"

Before she had a chance to answer, the road turned to the right, revealing the village of Snowsville. It was covered in fairy lights—and not just the trees. Every shop and house on the main street was strewn with them.

"Wow," she said, her bright, colorful stories giving way to reality. "It looks really beautiful."

Even as a man who didn't like Christmas, I couldn't argue with that. Along with the lights, the Christmas stalls were all covered in red velvet ribbons, which gave the market a different feel to Snowsly's, where each stallholder decorated the stall as they wanted—bar the meticulously placed lights.

"I'm beginning to think this isn't such a great idea. What if we get caught? And what if Snowsville's market is so good, it sends me spiraling?"

"If we get caught, we get sent to a South American prison for a couple of years. No big deal." A small smile curled around her lips. "And I won't let you spiral. Trust me. Come on," I said, pointing out a parking space. "Let's *snow* and be two different people for a couple of hours."

Her smile shined brighter than the fairy lights. "*Snow* time like the present."

TWELVE

Sebastian

After a little wrestle with Celia's Mini, I managed to extract myself. I held out my arm to her and she took it.

"You're right," she said. "No way we're going to get caught. You don't look like you're from around here."

I wasn't sure if I should be offended. Where did I look like I came from? Mars?

"Said the elfin princess who can't stop Christmas punning."

"But my hair is covered," she said, reaching around her hat to check that nothing had escaped.

"People aren't going to be on the lookout for spies from the next village," I said. "They're going to be focused on having a good time and making money."

This time, it was her turn to give me a cynical eye roll.

We wandered up the road. There weren't as many stalls as Snowsly had, and rather than them being set up on the smallish green, one of the roads toward the top of the hill had been closed off and lined with huts.

Celia was definitely jumpier than usual, and I couldn't tell if it was just excitement or if she was really nervous about being caught snooping.

"Shall we get our sea legs by getting a cup of hot chocolate?" I nodded toward the cart set up at the top of the road.

"You think they'll add a dash of brandy if I ask them nicely?"

We wandered over to the stall, greeted the Santa-hatted hot chocolate seller, and placed our order.

He placed two cardboard cups on a barrel upended by the side of the cart. "You come far?" he asked.

"We're on a mini-moon," Celia blurted. "Like a honeymoon but smaller. We're newlyweds. We've come from Oxford. Or just outside. A village called Wheatley."

The seller gave Celia a look that was somewhere between sympathy and suspicion. I pressed a kiss to the top of her head in an effort to calm her.

"You live here?" I asked the vendor before Celia had given the poor guy a rundown of our entire, invented, life story.

"Moreton," he replied. "Help yourself to mini marshmallows."

Celia scooped a spoonful into my cup and then into her own. "Thank you," Celia called over her shoulder. Then to me, under her breath, "Do you think he suspected anything? The kiss on my head was inspired." She grinned up at me, and I had to hold back from pulling her into my arms and kissing her properly. Maybe later.

"I'm not sure you need to offer quite so much information. Lying isn't top of my skill set, but if people aren't asking questions, there's no need to provide answers."

"You're right. I'm a maniac." She sighed before taking a

sip of her hot chocolate. "At least my punning seems to be under control. Sometimes it takes on a life of its own."

"Long may the hiatus last." I lifted my arm and she grinned, hooking hers underneath. I was unexpectedly enjoying the feeling that we were together here, alone, pretending to be a couple.

"This hot chocolate has nothing on Howard's," she said as we headed toward the start of the market.

I didn't point out that what we were drinking was also ninety-nine percent less likely to be a contributor to a cardiac arrest.

The first stall we came to sold wooden toys and advent calendars.

Celia frowned. "I don't recognize these stalls being shops in Snowsville. But then Snowsville doesn't have that many shops . . ."

I guided us over to look at the wooden toys. Some painted, some just oiled or waxed. Many of them were Christmas decorations.

"Oh that cuckoo clock is absolutely darling," Celia said. I followed her gaze up to a brightly colored wooden house on the wall.

"It's actually a Christmas-themed German Black Forest weather house," the woman behind the counter, also wearing a Santa hat, said. "Mrs. Claus comes out when it's dry and Santa comes out when it's humid." The tiny A-framed house had a door either side of a candy-cane pole. One side had Santa in the doorway, the other had Mrs. Claus. Out on the decking stood an array of animals that seemed to be sniffing at something under a Christmas tree. It was certainly very festive. And therefore a Celia magnet.

"Oh I see the thermometer now," Celia said. "It's so sweet. And it has the Christmas tree and the reindeer and everything." Celia was almost bouncing with excitement beside me.

"Are you local?" I asked.

The storekeeper shook her head. "Reading. I'm making the rounds of the Christmas markets. Only here tonight and then onto Bath for eight nights, then I'm done for the season."

Celia was still mesmerized by the weather house. "Is it *very* expensive?"

"A hundred and twenty-five, but I could sell it to you for a hundred and fifteen."

Celia deflated next to me. "It's so beautiful," she said, disappointment punctuating her words. "Maybe next year."

I led Celia away from the stall. "Have you made a pledge not to buy any more Christmas decorations?" I asked. "I imagine your place is quite a grotto. Maybe you should open it up to the public next year and charge an entry fee."

She tugged on my arm and forced her mouth into a smile. "It's not completely overrun, but you know how I enjoy the season. I just can't justify a purchase like that. Even for something so unusual."

She couldn't afford it. I might hate Christmas, but I hated seeing Celia disappointed more. I wanted to march us both back over there to buy it for her. What was happening to me?

"Well, if you change your mind, she's in Bath the day after tomorrow."

"She is? I didn't hear her say that. So it's not just local shops that have stalls. Is that a disadvantage or an advantage?"

"It's something Snowsly could experiment with. Maybe pick a few, select vendors from outside the village."

Celia's eyes widened and she reached and pressed a finger on my lips. "You're going to give us away."

I laughed, tugging her hand down. "If you're so worried . . ." I cupped her face in my hands, smoothing my thumb over her cheek. "Maybe I should kiss you again."

I could feel her blush under my fingers.

"Oh, I'm *very* worried. *Terrified.*"

I chuckled then pressed a kiss onto her lips. She was just as warm as I remembered, just as soft as she had been the first time. Desire stirred in my stomach. As I went to step back, she grabbed the front of my coat, pulling me toward her, and slid her tongue between my lips. I groaned as I deepened our kiss, not thinking about anything but how she felt, how she tasted, and how my desire started to slink down my limbs, warming my entire body.

"That was very convincing," she whispered breathily as our lips parted.

I kissed her again on the top of her head and offered her my arm, in no rush to get back to Snowsly anytime soon.

We wandered through the row of Christmas stalls, including one place selling nothing but gloves. Celia tried and failed to make me purchase a pair. At the end of the run, Celia stood on tiptoes and whispered into my ear. "I've had an idea. We should get elf costumes. Really good ones."

"You and me? Now?" I grinned at her.

She rolled her eyes. "I'm not sure you'd cut it as an elfin prince."

I clutched at my chest. "A devastating blow."

"We could have people dress up at the market. You know, like at Disney. Children will want to come to the village and meet them all."

She'd been having lots of these ideas as we wandered

around the market. And they were mostly good, excepting her notion to bring live reindeer onto the village green.

"And have their pictures taken," I added. "Even set up a festive backdrop to take the pictures in front of. Social media is going to be key to attracting people."

"Oh yes!" She squeezed my arm. "We could do a treasure hunt with a map and note all the photo opportunities on it." That was a great idea. I couldn't help but think that if she didn't like her job, she'd be good at just about anything she set her mind to. "Ohhh, look. We should definitely try the mulled wine. They have a non-alcoholic version. That's a great idea when people are driving into the village. I have to remember to tell Oliver."

We took our places in the queue. Celia tried to stand on tiptoes. "I wonder if I know who's manning the stall. I don't want to . . ." Her voice melted into the chatter of the crowd as I tuned into a once-familiar sound—a piece of music I couldn't quite place. All I knew for sure was that I hadn't heard it for a very long time.

"I'm going to check something out. I'll meet you back here," I said as I stepped away from Celia and followed the recognizable melody.

As I retraced our steps, I discovered a smaller stall at right angles to a stall selling woolen gloves. As soon as I saw what they were selling, I knew instantly where I recognized the sound from.

My jaw clenched as I took in the wooden musical jewelry box that my mother had when I was a child.

It featured in some of my earliest memories.

"Would you like a look, sir?" the slight woman behind the counter said.

I nodded, and she set the square mahogany box with small ebony feet on a velvet-covered counter in front of me.

It was exactly the one my mother had. *Had* until my father had thrown it across their bedroom during one of their fights before they divorced. The box had splintered into hundreds of unrecognizable, irreparable pieces.

It was one of the only times I'd ever seen my mother full of sadness rather than rage. I tried to bat away the memory.

"It's the only one I've ever seen like it," the vendor said.

I lifted the lid to hear the familiar tune that had brought me here. Instantly, I was transported back to those unhappy times. Trying to stay out late so I didn't have to go home to the arguing. Refusing sleepovers with friends because I knew I could never return the invitation. Trying to convince Granny to let me live with her permanently.

Inside, the box was lined in burgundy velvet and divided into four small trays. Just like my mother's had been.

"I'll take it." I hadn't bought my mother a Christmas present since I was seventeen. But something inside me couldn't leave this box behind. I didn't know whether my mother had searched for one since hers had been smashed or why she'd been quite so devastated by its destruction, but I couldn't leave this here. It was like it belonged to her or me or our shared history or . . . something.

As I headed back to the mulled wine queue, I passed the stall selling the weather house. Celia had seemed so completely taken with it, I couldn't resist it a second time. "Can I take that, please?" I asked the seller. She beamed at me. "Your wife will be delighted."

I chuckled to myself. If only Celia knew how convincing we were as a couple, even when she didn't share our entire cover with total strangers. I wasn't going to tell her if it meant I wouldn't get to kiss her again.

About five seconds after I'd paid for the weather house

and had the parcel boxed, wrapped, and bagged in hand, I ran into Celia carrying two cups of mulled wine.

"You've been shopping. In Snowsville," she added tightly.

I laughed at her silent accusation of disloyalty. "I'm not allowed to buy my Secret Santa gift in Snowsly," I reminded her.

Her face softened and she glanced down at the box. I'd been able to fit the music box in one of my large inside pockets, but there was no hiding the weather house. "What is it?" she asked.

She was like an inquisitive puppy.

"You, of all people, should know I'm sworn to secrecy."

"Can you at least tell me who it's for?"

"I absolutely cannot do that. I'm not going to be responsible for ruining Christmas, and you shouldn't even be asking."

She rolled her eyes and thrust the cup of wine into my free hand. "I hope you choke on it," she said in mock fury. "Shall we go?"

I chuckled, enjoying her frustration more than I should. "Yup. We've seen everything we came to see. Let's head back to the car."

Hopefully the box would fit on the back seat because there was no way all three of us would fit in the front.

This time, I took off my coat and made it into the passenger seat with relative ease. Maybe it was the mulled wine or maybe the kiss that had loosened my limbs.

"For what it's worth, I think the Snowsly market is better," I said as Celia pushed her key into the ignition. "The stalls in Snowsville seem . . . not as cohesive somehow. Does this car have heating? It's really cold in here."

Celia glanced at me, panic in her expression. "Sebastian, I'm turning the key."

Fair point—I was being impatient. "Sorry, I—"

"No, I mean I'm turning the key and nothing is happening."

Realization dawned. "The engine is dead?"

"I turned off the lights. I swear I did."

"It's not making any sound?"

"No. It's the battery. It must be. I can't have flooded it when I've not even been able to turn the engine over. Unless . . . Oh, no. You think someone spotted us and messed with the engine?"

I burst into laughter. "No, I don't think people have sabotaged your ninety-year-old car because we came to a neighboring village's Christmas market. Your imagination and creativity are an asset to you, Celia. But sometimes you need to rein it in."

"Yeah, that probably didn't happen," she conceded. "It wasn't like we really needed the cover stories we invented."

"*You* invented. Leave me out of it, although the kissing part was more than acceptable," I replied. "But look." I pointed to the road ahead. "Your lights are on. It can't be the battery." I scanned the dashboard. "It looks like your petrol is empty."

"No, there's no way. I filled her up two days ago and have only used her once to go to the supermarket. The dial thing must be faulty."

It didn't matter at this moment why the car had broken down. We just needed to find some transportation. "So, do you have the name of a local taxi firm?"

Now it was Celia's time to laugh. "Around here? You're kidding. There are a couple of cabs in Moreton, but they won't come out here at this time of night."

"What, we can't find a cab at all? What about an all-night garage?"

"No, the nearest garage is the one I use at Chipping Camden. Or there might be one at Winchcombe, but nothing's going to be open now." She fumbled for her phone. "It's just gone ten. We're going to have to call someone in the village and ask them to come and get us."

I opened the door of the Mini. "Let's go to the pub before it shuts. At least it will be somewhere to wait in the warm. We'll freeze if we stay out here."

Celia followed me out of the car. "I'm going to try Howard. He has a Land Rover. It's icy out there tonight." As we walked back up hill to the Black Swan, Celia tried to get in contact with Howard.

"I'm not getting any answer from Howard, Barbara's going straight to voicemail, and I must have the wrong number for Jim. It says the number isn't recognized. I don't have a number for Keely or Peter. I'm going to try the Manor. See if anyone's around."

We got to the bar in the Black Swan just a few minutes before last orders. It was almost deserted. There was one older guy on a stool at the bar and a middle-aged couple by the fireplace. That was it. While the bartender started preparing the hot toddies I'd ordered, Celia was still buried in her phone.

"Fiona's on her own in reception so she can't go and find anyone. Where did everyone disappear to? There are always people around. I guess we'll have to walk it."

Celia had lost her mind if she thought we were walking back to Snowsly. "We're not walking anywhere, particularly somewhere six miles away in sub-zero temperatures. We'll ask someone for a lift. Maybe the barman here. I can offer them some cash. It'll be fine."

Celia turned to me, looking like I'd just told her I was planning to murder her cat. "Promise me there is no way on this planet that you're going to do that. We can't blow our cover. Not at this point."

"Because?" I was almost certain no one would care that we'd come from Snowsly, but even if they did, so what? "What's the worst that can happen?" I wasn't going to be talked into making a freezing-cold trek on pitch black roads when I could just ask someone for a lift.

"We're having car trouble, mate," I said to the barman as he slid our two drinks toward me. "Any chance of a lift to the next village when you've finished your shift? I'll make it worth your while."

"Sorry. No car. Haven't even got a license. I cycle everywhere."

Shit.

"Stay here," I said to Celia as I stalked toward the couple by the fireplace.

"We've shared a bottle of wine," the woman said after I'd explained our situation. "There's no way either of us can drive, otherwise we'd have been happy to take you both. We're staying upstairs for our anniversary so we can enjoy a few drinks."

I thanked them and turned away before it hit me and I turned back to them. "Upstairs? Do they have rooms?" Snowsville wasn't large enough for a hotel, but it made sense there'd be a few rooms above the pub.

"Only three. But they're all very nice."

I nodded and sped back to the bar. "You have a couple of rooms available?" I asked, without consulting Celia.

"Just one," he said. "The Cygnet room."

"We'll take it."

I handed over my credit card and paid in full, ignoring Celia's insistent tug on my coat.

"I'll get the key," the barman said.

"Are you serious?" she said through her smile as he disappeared. "We can't stay the night! We're bound to get busted if they see me in daylight."

I chuckled. I thought she was going to have a problem with sharing a room, not blowing our cover.

"It will be fine," I said. "We'll get someone to pick us up in the morning from the back door. No one will see a thing. I reckon they could smuggle Madonna out of here first thing and no one would be any the wiser."

"And one room?"

I shrugged. "They only had one room. And the Marriot next door is fully booked."

The barman came back with our key and pointed us in the direction of the stairs.

"Come on, Mrs. Fox. I'll carry you over the threshold if you're lucky."

Celia squealed as I reached to pick her up, a bloom in her cheeks appearing that was impossible to miss. I relented, stopped trying to pick her up, and followed her up the stairs.

Our room was clean and comfortable—not as big as the Blue Room back at the Manor, but there was plenty of room to lay our heads for a few hours until someone picked up their phone.

"You're right, this really was our only option," Celia said, flopping down into the flowery chair behind the door. "I can sleep in the chair."

The chair?

There was no way I was going to let Celia take the chair. "Take the bed. It's late. You've been working every daylight hour and a lot of the ones in darkness, too."

"You've been working just as hard as me. *You* paid for the room. *And* I got us into this mess. Anyway, I'm better suited to the chair. I'm used to flying economy on planes. No doubt, you're up in first class with your big, fancy beds and cashmere blankets."

I laughed at her assumption—which wasn't wrong—and also at the way she was being so prim and proper about our sleeping arrangements. We weren't strangers and we weren't in the eighteenth century. We were two adults sharing a bedroom. It wasn't a big deal if she didn't want it to be. We'd kissed, her infectious enthusiasm for Christmas was burrowing into my heart, and I'd like to kiss her again in the private warmth of our hotel room. Still, I didn't want her to feel uncomfortable.

"Well, how about this for a radical idea: We can both take the bed. It's a big bed—plenty of room for both of us. If you feel uncomfortable, I'll stay on top of the covers. And we can both stay fully clothed. How about that?" I'd be content with option A, but an option B where neither of us were wearing anything and we were on top of the covers, underneath the covers, against the door, and bent over the bath would work too.

She pulled off her hat and toed off her boots. "I had such a lovely time tonight and now everything's ruined because of my ninety-year-old car."

"It's not ruined," I said, taking a seat on the bed to unlace my shoes. "The bad can't undo the good like that. Not unless you let it."

She sighed like she'd just missed a flight or something. "I'm going to pay you back for the room as soon as I get paid at the end of the month. This is all my fault."

Of all the things she was worried about, it was how to pay for the room? The look in her eyes made me want to fix things so she didn't feel bad about anything ever again. I'd go and buy her a new car and the bloody hotel if it made her feel better. "I'd be offended if you offered me money."

"Really?"

"Well, not *offended*. But I wouldn't accept it. This is no one's fault. And we don't have to let it ruin a fun evening."

"You had fun?" Her tone brightened and her eyes lit up. "Sebastian, listen to yourself—you *enjoyed* yourself. At a Christmas market. I just knew that being in Snowsly during the festive season would change your mind about this time of year."

Didn't she realize it wasn't the merriness and good will of the Snowsville Christmas market that had shifted my mood from surly to bordering on cheerful? It was her. "I'm finding it increasingly difficult *not* to have fun when I'm with you."

She tilted her head as she gave me a small smile. "What was the funnest bit?"

"Are you fishing for compliments, Celia Sommers?" I scooted around the bed to face her so our knees were touching. "Do you want me to tell you how much I enjoyed kissing you? How I want to kiss you again? How we have plenty of time for lots more kissing?"

She drew a circle on my knee. "Maybe a little. But also, a few days ago you would never have had fun at a Christmas market. I like hearing that you're in a more festive mood."

"Why?" I asked, genuinely intrigued. Why did she care if I enjoyed Christmas?

"I want everyone to love it. I can't bear the thought of the people around me not being happy. How can Christmas be perfect if everyone's not happy?"

I'd gotten to know Celia over the last few days and I knew she wasn't some naïve girl who still believed in fairytales, but there was something about Christmas that had her on a mission. "But nothing's perfect," I said.

"Don't say that." She closed her eyes for one beat then two. When she opened them, her blue-blue eyes had that look I recognized. Like everything hinged on Christmas. Like everything hung in the balance. "This Christmas is going to be perfect. And it's going to erase every imperfect thing about last Christmas."

I reached out and brushed my thumb over her cheek-bone. "What happened last Christmas?"

THIRTEEN

Celia

The way Sebastian touched me—just with the lightest sweep of his fingers—made me wish, just for a second, that we were both wearing a lot less clothing. The way he'd dealt with my car breaking down and finding us a room—his taking control had been a relief. He was so sure he could find a solution that I believed he would. And he had. It felt freeing that I didn't have to take responsibility for absolutely everything. I could rely on Sebastian. Trust him. And I wasn't sure if was that or if it was his perfectly cut jaw and ice-blue eyes that had me hoping he wouldn't be sleeping on top of the covers tonight.

Sebastian pulled off his jumper and arranged himself on the bed, resting against the headboard, his legs crossed at the ankle. He patted the bed next to him, like he really wanted to hear what I had to say.

I moved around the bed and then lay on my side, my head propped up on my hand. "Last Christmas was . . . difficult. My boyfriend left me on Christmas Eve. I came home from checking on the market, wondering why he hadn't joined me as he said he was going to, to find his bags packed and already in his car. Our car." It was like the threads of my future had been trapped in the car door, and as he drove away, everything I thought was in store for me unraveled.

"I'm sorry," Sebastian said, his deep, silky voice winding around my body.

"Shitty timing," I said. "I'd thought he was building up to a proposal. We'd been talking about moving to a bigger place in the village. And he'd been asking Lemon about my ring size. And then . . . not. The exact opposite, in fact. It was just unexpected, that's all."

"He was an idiot."

It was a kind thing to say but I didn't believe it. "Maybe. It took the shine off the holidays last year, that's all." I'd spent Christmas Day and Boxing Day in bed, ignoring my phone and the numerous knocks on the door. I couldn't face anyone. I just wanted to forget that Christmas was happening. "I'm determined that the bad memories won't ruin every Christmas for me. This year, I want to make up for last year's lost Christmas—make new memories and consign last Christmas to a bin marked Do Not Open." I tried to make the words have a no-big-deal vibe about them, but even to me they came out flat and a little sad. The fact was, the closer Christmas Eve came, the more my desperation increased. I wasn't sure I could face another bad Christmas.

"Why did he leave?"

I blew out a breath. "I have no idea. He just said it wasn't working. I thought he'd go but we'd end up talking it through and eventually he'd come back, but none of that happened. Except the 'him going' part. We haven't spoken since he left."

"He was a coward." Sebastian paused as if he wanted to say more but didn't. "How long were you together?"

"Six years." I felt stupid every time I thought about it. How had he walked away so easily from a *six-year* relationship? "I thought I'd found the one. You know? I thought we'd get married, have babies, grow old in Snowsly. Guess life doesn't always go to plan."

"What a dick."

I forced a smile. "You sound like Lemon."

"What? Sour?"

I laughed and for a second all I wanted to do was kiss Sebastian. "My best friend's name is Lemon. *You're* not a lemon. She's always telling me Carl is an idiot, but if he was a dick all along, what does it say about me that I was planning a future with him?"

"It says nothing about you," he said, pushing my escaped hair back from my face. "No decent man leaves a woman without an explanation." He shifted so he was on his side opposite me. "You haven't heard from him since?"

I shook my head. "Six years, and all I have to show for it is a bin bag of discarded belongings."

"You still have his stuff?"

"The things he left behind," I clarified.

He drew his eyebrows together. "You haven't burned them or at least thrown them away?"

"Lemon says I need to get angry and do some ritual burning. But I'm not an angry person. I like life to be good. I want to be happy."

Sebastian looked at me, his lips pressed together, his brow furrowed. "Being angry doesn't have to make you an angry person. Anger can drive you forward, push you over the brow of whatever hill you're climbing."

I shrugged. That wasn't how I was wired. "You use anger like that?"

"I try to. Try to use it as fuel rather than have it control me, like it did my father." He shook his head. "His temper was legendary. He lost numerous jobs over it, not to mention friends and his wife."

"I'm sorry," I said.

"He died a long time ago. I was twenty. At his funeral, I remember thinking that I wouldn't let myself become him. I wouldn't let my anger control me like it had done him. But I still have it in me. I've just learnt to use it to make me better. That's the point, Celia. Don't pretend it's not there— because it's in all of us. Just direct it. Harness it. Use it. Setting fire to your arsehole-boyfriend's clothes might just set you free."

I laughed and cupped his face in my hand. "Thank you. Maybe I'll hire you to do it for me."

"So instead of getting angry and getting over him, you've decided that if this year's Christmas is perfect, it will make up for how thoroughly awful last year was for you?"

"I suppose. I need proof that what happened is in my past. That Christmas isn't a ruined holiday for me and I can look forward to good ones again going forward."

"In reality though, you know that one bad Christmas doesn't make them all bad, just like a broken-down car doesn't neutralize an evening with good company and a blistering array of Christmas puns."

I narrowed my eyes and tried not to smile. I knew he secretly loved my puns.

"So maybe it goes deeper than that," he said. "Are you trying to trick yourself into believing that *life* will get better if you have a good Christmas?"

Was that what I was about? "It's an anniversary of sorts.

Not just of Carl leaving but of what I thought was going to be my future going up in flames. Before, I was certain of how the next five years were going to go. For the last year, I've not known what direction I'm headed. Maybe a great Christmas will allow me to break free of this limbo I've been living for the last twelve months and move forward."

"You want the Christmas magic to show you your future," he said, putting together all the pieces of what I'd confessed. Even if it sounded ridiculous, which I was afraid it might, Sebastian didn't say so.

"Maybe." I'd always loved Christmas, but my appreciation of the season had shifted into a new gear this year. Sebastian was right. I was hoping for a Christmas miracle.

"Even if it felt like you had your life with Carl planned out, you didn't know for certain. You just *thought* you did. That certainty you had was just an illusion."

My heart thunked in my ribcage as if I'd done an emergency stop and it wasn't wearing a seatbelt. I sat up on the bed. I couldn't think straight lying down. I'd never thought about it that way, but Sebastian was right—my future had never been mapped out like I'd thought. Maybe at some point, Carl thought we'd be married too, but something had changed in him. His future shifted. Mine had too. "Our futures are always shifting," I said, almost to myself.

"Death and taxes are the only certain things in life, so Benjamin Franklin said."

The way Sebastian said it seemed so matter-of-fact, but it felt to me that he'd just explained quantum mechanics in a way that actually made sense.

"I suppose."

It was a Christmas miracle.

And Sebastian had made it happen.

Sebastian leapt to his feet. "Can I have your car keys? I need to get something."

I was still too busy processing the implications of what he'd just said to ask him where he was going. "Sure, they're on the dresser."

"I'll be two minutes."

"Sebastian, your coat," I called after him but it was too late. He was gone. Had I bored him?

I slumped back down on the pillow and texted Lemon. *Do I drive men away?*

A few minutes later, I got a reply. *You will do if you haven't burned your ex's stupid Star Wars duvet cover yet.*

A few minutes later, I jumped at the rattle of the door handle. Sebastian appeared in the doorway, carrying the box for his Secret Santa.

"Here," he said, kicking the door closed with his foot and then stalking over to where I sat on the bed. "Open it."

"That's for your Secret Santa person."

He sat down at the foot of the bed. "*You're* my Secret Santa person. And I want you to open it."

My heart inched higher in my chest. I was desperate to know what he'd chosen, but I didn't want to break the rules.

"We're not meant to exchange gifts until Christmas Eve," I said, staring at the box, wondering if my x-ray vision was going to kick in anytime soon.

"Open it, Celia."

I rolled my lips together. Would it matter if I broke the rules, just this once?

I pulled the top flaps of the box open and peered inside, but cardboard covered whatever it was. When I finally uncovered it and saw what looked like tiny roofing tiles, I knew instantly what he'd done. The German Black Forest weather house. Nobody had ever bought me anything so wonderful.

"Sebastian." I was so touched. If I'd had the money, I'd have bought it for myself tonight. But I was also sort of sad because I knew Carl, the man I'd shared so much with and who I thought I was going to marry, never would have thought to buy me anything so perfect. "This was way over the twenty-pound limit."

He shrugged. "So shoot me."

I pulled out the house and set it on the bed. Sebastian took the cardboard box and put it over by the door before taking a seat on his side of the bed. There were so many details I'd not appreciated when I'd seen it on the shelf in the stall. "I hadn't even noticed one of the reindeer has a red nose. And the wood is so beautiful! It looks exactly like a house you might find in the Black Forest. Only shrunken."

"It's nice to see you smile."

The gruff grinch I'd met a few days ago had dissolved into a kind, caring man who I was lucky to have spent so much time with this last week. I moved off the bed and set the house on the dresser before rounding the bed to Sebastian's side. I sat next to where he was reclined on the pillow, my heart ping-ponging in my chest. "Thank you." I was barely able to get the words out, I was so overwhelmed at his gift—at him being so close, and being such a good listener, and the way he made me see me better than I saw myself. I leaned forward and pressed a kiss on his cheek. "It's incredibly generous of you. And . . . I couldn't be more grateful."

He sat upright, our faces just centimeters apart, our breaths sweeping across each other's cheeks. The scent of nutmeg and fire filled my lungs. "I know a German Black Forest house won't make what he did any better but—"

I pressed my lips to his. I just couldn't help it. He

smelled so good, and he'd been so kind and patient and open. Not to mention he might just be the most handsome man I'd ever laid eyes on.

Just as I began to sink into his kiss, he pulled back. "The gift doesn't need repaying. I didn't bring it in from the car in the hope that it would lead to anything." He shook his head. "I should have left it where it was. I just . . . don't like seeing you sad."

He didn't like seeing me sad? He had the direct dial to my ovaries. "Sebastian, I can't imagine you'd ever have to give any woman a gift in exchange for a kiss. I'm sure women are queuing down the street for a kiss from you. And rightly so. That kiss wasn't repayment. I'm kissing you because I want to kiss you."

His eyes darkened. "I want to kiss you too." He cupped the back of my neck and pulled me toward him, took my bottom lip between his and groaned. Goosebumps sheeted my skin and I ran my hands up his chest. He was all hard muscles under soft wool and I wanted to curl up on him and sleep until Christmas. And I wanted to strip him naked and trace each ab with my tongue.

With a sigh, he pulled back. "I've wanted to do that again since I last kissed you."

I smiled. "What took you so long?"

He laughed and leaned forward, placing a small kiss on the corner of my lip. "You're funny. And cute." He pressed a kiss on the opposite side of my mouth. "And sexy."

I pushed my hands up under his untucked, cotton shirt. "You're *so* sexy," I said, guiding the jumper up. Our eyes met and he took over, stripping off his top.

Fate had brought us here. The two of us. To a village where neither of us was ourselves for the night. I had nothing to lose and everything to gain.

I pressed a kiss at the juncture between his collarbones, just above the neck of his crisp, white t-shirt before stripping off my blue and white jumper.

"You're beautiful," he said, rolling me to my back and crawling on top of me, inching up my t-shirt and pushing it up over my head. "But I have to admit, I'm a little disappointed that the Christmas theme doesn't extend to your underwear." He glanced down at my plain white bra.

"If it makes up for it, Santa's waiting in my jeans," I replied.

He chuckled. "Wow. Okay. I've never been into threesomes but for Santa, I'd have to make an exception." He tugged down my jeans and placed a kiss on my underwear, just over my clit, like he was putting me on notice of what was to come.

And I was here for it.

All of it.

I wanted to sink into tonight and enjoy Sebastian, forgetting the outside world for as long as we were together.

He trailed kisses up my inner thigh before stripping off my underwear and leaving me lying, totally naked, on the bed. He stood, his gaze travelling up and down my body like he was making a mental note of how the next however-long was going to go. He undressed, not rushing as he kept focused on me.

And I focused on him right back.

FOURTEEN

Sebastian

I didn't know where to start. She was like lush, ripe fruit that I wanted to sink my teeth into, suck, and feel drip down my chin. I grazed my lips over her breasts as she writhed and squirmed below me.

My cock was straining, desperate to bury deep into her, but I was going to wait. I wanted to explore her.

I swept my hands up her thighs, my thumbs hooking under her hip bones as I spread my fingers around her tiny waist. Her wet pussy almost dared me to dip down and take a taste, but I wanted a few minutes just to enjoy the sight of her before I feasted.

"Sebastian, are you going to torture me?"

The corners of my mouth flickered in response. "Maybe a little."

She sighed and closed her eyes and I began to make my way up her body, pressing small, chaste kisses against her snow-soft skin. I started at her ankles, moving up as I desperately tried to quench my thirst for her by exploring every inch of her incredible, gorgeous body.

As I got to the top her thighs, she tensed. I pressed another innocent kiss on her mound and she exhaled as I lulled her into a false sense of security.

Without warning, I changed tack. Instead of continuing my climb up her body, I dipped my tongue into her slit, circling her clit, finding her deliciously wet. She was sweet inside and out, and my cock reared in appreciation. I pushed her thighs wide and covered her with my mouth, sucking and licking, pushing my tongue inside her and running it up and down her folds.

"It's so good," she huffed out. "So, so, so, so good."

Pride mixed with relief that I was able to make her feel good—as good as I felt when I was around her. She'd been entirely unexpected and had made my trip to Snowsly not just bearable but enjoyable. As I pressed my tongue deeper and rounded her clit with my thumb, she pulled a pillow onto her face and groaned into it. She began to shiver, her legs vibrating as if whatever she was feeling inside was spilling out. She was joyously responsive, and when she tensed and called out my name into the pillow, I made gentle, soothing strokes with my tongue over her pulsing clit.

"That tongue," she croaked out, her arm flopped across her face, the pillow falling onto the floor.

I stood and pulled a condom from my wallet. Christ, I was so hard for her now. So fucking ready to bury myself in her. I knew I had to be patient, but I was so full with lust I could hardly see straight. It was going to take until *next* Christmas to do all the things I wanted to do to her.

She pushed up on her elbows, her perfect breasts undulating as if they knew the effect they had on me and were trying to reciprocate their own kind of torture. Then she drew up her legs and sat upright. Cross legged. "It seems only fair before we use that . . ." She nodded toward the condom that I was about to tear open. "That I get to taste you."

It was my turn to groan. I bent, placed a greedy kiss on her lips and straightened, my cock straining painfully. I was going to have to sing "Twelve Days of Christmas" to myself if I didn't want to erupt into her as soon as her lips touched my crown.

She didn't seem to be in a rush to move and I realized she was fiddling with the unusual double plait she wore her hair in. "You mind if I take this down?"

It was official. She was trying to kill me.

With a final tug, her white-blonde tresses fell like a curtain around her.

"So beautiful," I said, shaking my head, almost incredulous.

She shifted, her hair trailing after her as she positioned her back to me. Then she laid herself down, her head off the end of the mattress, that glorious hair falling like a silken sheet down the side of the bed. Then she tipped her chin back, mouth open. Ready for my cock.

Jesus.

On the surface, Celia was all sweetness, but apparently, after dark, she also deserved a place on the naughty list.

I almost shook with desire as I traced the head of my cock around her lips, then dipped in the crown, so just a hint of her heat seeped into me. I was going to have to take this slow—for my sake, not hers.

She reached behind me and found the backs of my thighs. And *pushed*.

My vision blurred and I fell forward, bracing myself on

the mattress as she swallowed my cock deep into her throat. I was a fraction of a second from coming before I withdrew and tried to steady my scrambling heart rate.

Then she opened her legs and rocketed right to the top of the naughty list.

Fuck.

I could see her wetness, feel her tongue dancing on my crown, smell her delicious, sweet scent of fire and forest. I gave up control to my animal instincts. There would be no holding back with Celia.

My fingers went to work, alternately pushing into her and trailing her folds, all while my hips levered back and forward, driving my cock into her mouth. I reveled in her tongue, firm and soft against my shaft. My fingers were wet with her desire for me. Her fingertips dug into my arse, urging me deeper.

It was a fucking wonderland.

A fucking Christmas wonderland.

"I'm going to come," I coughed out, wanting to maintain this blissful blur of pleasure but knowing that something so hot, so bright, so completely fucking intense couldn't last long.

Her hips pushed off the bed as she began to shake, coming around my fingers as I emptied myself onto her tongue.

Fuck, was it wrong to know that this image of her right here, open beneath me, was going to stay with me until all the Christmases in the world had been used up?

"For someone who likes Christmas and the cold so much, you're ridiculously hot." I pulled her up into my arms and lay us both back on the pillows to catch our breath.

"For someone who pretends to be so cold, you've got a really nice penis."

I laughed. "Well, if anything could thaw me out, a night like this could. With you. You're all fire, Celia Sommers."

"Fire? I don't think so."

"*Burning* hot fire."

"Maybe just with you."

I loved that idea—that she'd saved her fire for me. That I was the man who encouraged her to be the scorching hot woman in my arms. I tightened my grip around her and we lay in comfortable silence.

"Thank you again for the weather house," she said after a couple of minutes. "I know it's breaking the twenty-pound rule but I don't even care. I love it so much."

It was such a small thing. Who knew it could bring so much joy? "I'm glad. I'll have to get you something else so I have something to hand over on Christmas Eve."

"If anyone knew what you'd given me this year, not only would they blush, but they certainly wouldn't mind you being empty-handed on Christmas Eve. I know you came up to help Ivy, but I don't know what I would have done without you. You've been the perfect partner in crime."

I smoothed my hand down her arm. "You'd have Christmas at Snowsly handled with or without me, but I'm pleased to be able to help." I'd had more fun that I'd thought possible, and I hadn't been dogged with too many bad memories. Not yet, anyway.

"Not missing Barbados too much?"

"Not *too* much."

She pulled out of my arms, kneeled, and hooked a leg over my hips. "I'm going to have to turn that *not too much* into a *not at all.*"

I sighed, my body completely exhausted but entirely responsive to the naked, beautiful Celia astride me.

I swept her hair over her shoulder, the silky strands pouring over her like cream. "You're insatiable."

"In just a few days, you'll be gone. I need to make the most of you."

She leaned over to get the condom on the bedside table and I took it from her. I'd be quicker and I wanted her on my cock, bucking and moaning as soon as possible. I wanted to see the Celia reserved just for me.

She melted onto my dick like ice in the sun, settling low so I was deep inside her. I had to remind myself to breathe.

How had any man who really knew how delicate and delectable, how fierce and fervent Celia really was, been fool enough to leave her?

She rocked her hips a little, back and forth, keeping me deep, keeping us close. She swept her fingers over my forehead. "You think too much."

I cupped her breasts, flicking her nipples with my thumbs and she bucked under my touch, sending waves of pleasure into my stomach like a rising tide. Then she started to move, the undulating waves of the sea rocking against the shore. Her tightness surrounding me, pulling me in deep. All I could do was watch her wide mouth as she panted through her pleasure. All I could do was breathe in her magic.

She hooked her hands over my shoulders like she was losing strength, or maybe she was just as overwhelmed by how good it all felt as I was. I lifted her chin, sat up, and pressed my lips to hers, my tongue pressing between her lips, tasting and taking more and more. The energy shifted between us and the need for *more* kept calling, a voice growing louder with every passing moment. I needed to take more, more, more. I needed to give more, more, more.

I clasped her waist and began to move her, driving her

back and forth on my cock. She met every one of my grunts and moans with a sound of her own. Every *oh yes, right there* and *please don't stop*. I devoured each one.

Face-to-face, I'd never felt so intimate with someone, never felt so close to another human being in all of my life. I'd known this woman for just a few days, but it was as if tonight a curtain had lifted and I'd discovered I'd known her my entire life. I'd never felt so completely comfortable, so completely complete, as I did in this moment with Celia.

Her breaths were coming fast and heavy, like she was about to reach the summit of the mountain but was chasing sunset and had to get there as fast as possible. Her cheeks, neck, and chest were flushed from exertion. Slick heat urged us faster.

Fuck, she was beautiful.

I pulled her down on my cock, less controlled and more haphazard now as my instinct to come took over. Jesus, I couldn't get close enough to her.

I needed more.

For longer.

I needed everything from her.

I flipped us over so she was on her back and I drove into her, giving her all I had in that moment, trying to make it even better between us. I felt her orgasm approach in the second that she did and I upped my pace. Her hands reached around her for a pillow, but they were all kicked to the floor, so I covered her mouth with my hand. The moment my palm slid into place, she screamed her climax, howling my name into my skin. I relentlessly fucked her through her climax, determined to hold onto this perfect evening for as long as I could.

I didn't stop. Didn't slow. Not for a second.

I fucked and fucked until sweat dripped from my chest onto hers and her limp body began to shake again.

"I think I might break . . ." She panted out the words like she wasn't sure if she could get them out. "If I come like that again."

I shook my head, my ears ringing, tendons strained, muscles aching from needing this so much and getting it all. "I'm going to hold you together and we're both going to break at the same time."

I could feel every beat, every pulse, every throb of our bodies. I didn't know where I ended and she began.

Her fingernails bit into my shoulders. We both knew we were almost where we needed to be. My climax growled to life at the base of my spine like a shot of adrenaline directly into my heart.

"Sebastian," she called, a warning. I had to be careful. Somehow, this meant too much not to savor every last drop. Instead of using my hand, I covered her mouth with mine. A tremor passed through our bodies and we came holding each other, no space in between.

FIFTEEN

Celia

At some point the night before, I must have fallen asleep. Or passed out. I woke to the echo of a thousand fingerprints all over my body, courtesy of Sebastian's hands. I opened my eyes to find my phone's screen flashing with Howard's name.

I bolted upright and accepted the call.

"Everything okay?" he asked. "I got a late call from you last night."

"Yes. No. My car broke down. We've been stranded in Snowsville all night. We need a lift. Or a tow or something. We had to stay overnight at the Black Swan." I resisted the urge to over-explain.

There was only one room left.

We were forced to share.

I said I'd take the chair.

But why? Howard didn't care, and Sebastian and I were both single. It just felt a little weird because in Snowsly, they'd only ever known me as Celia and Carl. And then just Celia.

"I'm on my way. I can tow you. We'll get you back. See you in twenty minutes."

"Thanks, Howard. See you soon."

I turned to find Sebastian stretching languidly, like a big cat in the sun. "That was Howard." I swung my legs over the bed.

"I guessed, seeing as you just called him Howard."

"Did you just make a joke? My cup runneth over. But seriously, we've got twenty minutes."

He growled, reached for me and pulled my naked body against his. He was a mixture of hard and soft, and his fingertips on my arse and his tongue on my neck threatened to pull me under. "It's not long enough. I need you in this bed until at least New Year."

I pulled out of his arms, feigning exasperation. The truth was, I wanted him too. I'd begun to worry that I'd never get enough, which was a problem, given he'd be gone by Christmas. I pushed the thought aside, determined not to fall into a panic spiral about a pattern of men leaving me on December twenty-fourth. "As much as that sounds like fun, I don't want to greet Howard at the door naked. I'm getting a quick shower."

"Need company?"

I grinned at him. "Yes, but we don't have time."

My phone buzzed again with a text from Keely. "And the hits just keep on coming. They've moved the Christmas Committee meeting to this morning at eight."

Howard made it to Snowsville in eighteen minutes. I was barely out of the shower and Sebastian was barely dressed. It was like Howard had been waiting for my call.

We crashed into the morning Christmas Committee meeting just two minutes late.

"Our wanderers return," Ivy said, her eyes bright with questions. "Don't worry, Howard told Barbara everything. It's time you got a new car, Celia."

"I'll check it out," Howard said. "You might just need some petrol."

Had I mentioned to Howard that the petrol gauge read empty? Maybe Sebastian had. I'd been in my car while he and Sebastian had sat with Howard.

"Good job the Black Swan had vacancies," Ivy said, a mischievous smile on her face. "So tell us, what's our competition doing?"

Once we'd delivered our Snowsville debrief, Cindy on reception interrupted with a large square package wrapped in layers of brown paper.

"For Sebastian," she said.

"Ahhh, I've been waiting for this," he said. "If you checked your email this morning, you'd have seen I circulated a logo and branded graphics for the market. I've sent it to all the shops in the village to use in their newsletters and have requested they send something out today if possible. It will give them a good reason to contact their customers, which may well lead to increased sales either online or through in-person attendance. A win for everyone" He tore open the brown paper parcel to reveal a sign for Christmas in Snowsly. As he held it up, I couldn't help but think how ludicrous it looked—not the sign, that was beautiful. But Sebastian, the man who hated Christmas, holding up a red, green, and white sign covered with elves popping their heads around the letters, and Santa feeding his reindeer at the bottom.

"It's so festive," Ivy said, clearly delighted.

"I love the vintage feel," I said, peering closer. "It looks like it could have been from the fifties." It was perfect for Snowsly—cosy and friendly and inviting.

"People don't come to the Cotswolds for clean, modern lines. We've tried to keep it in keeping. Later today, smaller signs will arrive that can be put up on each stall. I want to run with Celia's idea and have some of my marketing team coming up later today to set up a couple of Instagram points —picture stations—that will encourage people to post on social media and spread the word."

Sebastian didn't waste time. I had no idea he was so invested.

"Sounds like Snowsville were doing some exciting stuff," Barbara said. "Have we any hope of holding on to at least some of our customers?" She sounded desperate.

"They have a lot of people from outside the village running stalls. We should consider that for next year, so we can attract an even wider audience with a bigger market. Vendors from outside the village have their own following, so we might capture the attention of people who've never visited us before."

"The village can charge for a stall and get additional income, too," Sebastian said.

I hadn't thought of charging the stallholders, but it would be great to cover some costs of the lighting and the stall itself. Even better.

"Nothing that would directly compete with any of our home-grown stallholders, of course. But there was one stall selling cuckoo clocks and beautiful German weather houses that were just delightful." I blushed thinking of the gift Sebastian had bought me. "And another selling festive shortbread. I also think it might be a good idea to have Christmas characters mingling with the crowd and taking pictures with visitors. Almost like the ones at Disneyland, but Christmas-themed. Like elves and Santa and stuff."

Murmurs of understanding and agreement tumbled through the group.

"We just have to keep our nerve," I said. "These new ideas will make Snowsly even more of a Christmas destination than it was before."

"Which reminds me," Sebastian said. "Celia, I've taken your idea about having Christmas characters and run with it. I've hired some elves to stroll through the market, greet the children, and take photographs. They'll arrive just before noon."

That was fast work. No wonder he was so successful in business. He knew how to get things done.

"I just sent a few messages on the drive back," he whispered, reading my mind. "One more thing," Sebastian added, addressing the room again. "Tomorrow afternoon, there's a journalist from *Good Housekeeping* and another from *Rallegra* magazine coming over to cover the market."

"A journalist?" Howard asked. "What on earth for?"

"To get Snowsly coverage," Ivy explained. "It's one thing to ensure Snowsly's the best Christmas market in the whole of Great Britain, but we've got to make sure people know about it." She turned to Sebastian. "You're a darling boy. Thank you."

Sebastian shrugged off the blush that crawled up from his collar. "Hopefully, with all these changes, we should see an impact on footfall and profits should start to go up. If this year doesn't turn around as quickly as we'd like, the publicity and branding should mean that we go into next year really strong."

If I didn't want to bang Sebastian before this meeting—which I totally did—I absolutely, one hundred percent wanted to strip him naked and mount him like a horse after what he'd just said and done. He was even sexier than usual when he was taking control and making things happen.

He turned to me and lowered his voice. "You're not offended that I implemented your ideas? You're brilliant, Celia—I just wanted to see your visions come to life."

"Not at all," I replied. "I'm so happy you did." It took all my willpower not to crawl into his lap and kiss him.

Whoever would have thought the Christmas-hating, Barbados-bound grinch might have just saved Christmas?

SIXTEEN

Celia

I wasn't sure if it was the fact that I hadn't had much sleep the previous night, or whether it was because I'd barely stopped for breath today, but I was exhausted.

I pulled on my reindeer pajamas and switched on the kettle. Some hot chocolate while I worked on my next idea might keep me awake. I pulled out the large box of unused decorations from under the stairs. I could have sworn the Santa costume from a few years back was in there. I reached down and grabbed something furry. This was it, or else a cat had crawled in and died here. I pulled my arm out and did a little jump when it came to the surface all red and Santa-like.

My phone buzzed with a text from Sebastian, offering to walk me home. For someone so grumpy, he really was very sweet. I texted back, telling him I'd headed home already. I'd barely spoken to him all day as we ran around, attaching the *Christmas in Snowsly* signs to the stalls, creating the Instagram stations, and making sure everything was as festive as possible in time for our visitors tomorrow. Snowsly's Christmas market was going to be on the *Good freaking Housekeeping* Instagram grid, and on *Rallegra's* website. Everything had to be more than perfect.

Now I just had to find needle and thread, and get to work sewing the white fur trim back onto Santa's coat. If I turned up to tomorrow's committee meeting with the costume, I was hopeful Howard might offer to play the role he was born for.

A knock at the door made me jump. I glanced down at my Rudolph pajamas. Whoever was at the door would just have to understand that I was one hundred percent myself.

I opened the door to a grinning Sebastian. His eyes dipped down to my chest. "You came home to be alone with Rudolph?"

One hundred percent myself.

"What can I say? He's great in bed."

He grinned, an unselfconscious, boyish grin I'd not seen on him before. It suited him.

"I'm making hot chocolate. You want some?"

"Does it have brandy in it?" He seemed more relaxed than usual. Maybe it was because we'd slept together. Last night I'd felt so connected to him—physically, but also more than that. I'd gotten to know the man beneath the grinch.

"ANOTHER FABULOUS IDEA." I led him through to my kitchen, and offered him a seat on one of the mismatched, brightly colored kitchen chairs gathered around the old pine table.

"Do you have a guest?" he asked, picking up the edge of the Santa costume. "Or are you secretly Santa?"

"I was hoping you might want to dress up."

He tried to suppress a laugh and took a seat. "And what's your costume? Naughty elf?"

This Sebastian was the one I saw last night—funny, kind, and sexy as hell.

Completely irresistible.

I abandoned the idea of hot chocolate and took a seat on his lap, linking my arms around his neck.

"It's quite the grotto in here." He threaded his arms around my waist and glanced around at the miniature Christmas tree on the work surface, my Christmas place-mats, the garlands along the tops of the cupboards, and the family of large felt penguins sporting Santa hats in the middle of the table.

Carl had always put his foot down when it came to decorating the kitchen. This year, I'd done what I wanted.

"I suppose it's a little over the top. My ex didn't approve."

"Well given he's your ex, that doesn't matter. If it makes you happy, you shouldn't care what anyone else thinks."

I turned to face him. Sebastian hated Christmas, but he didn't judge me for loving it. "Thank you," I said, snaking my arms around his waist. My hand hit something hard. "Do you have a brick in your pocket or are you just pleased to see me?"

Sebastian frowned and I tapped whatever it was he was storing in his ginormous pockets. "Oh," he said, reaching inside. "I bought this yesterday in Snowsville. I'd forgotten it was in there." He reached into his coat and pulled out a bubble-wrapped cube.

"What is it?"

He sighed. "I'm not sure."

"You bought it not knowing what it is?"

He leaned forward and I slipped off his lap and onto the

chair next to him. In a rare show of insecurity, he worried the tape holding the bubble wrap in place. "It's a music box. I'm just not quite sure what I'm going to do with it." His frown deepened as if he was having to decide whether or not to hand over state secrets.

The kettle snapped off and I stood to make our drinks. "What are the options?"

He leaned back, stretching out his long, lean legs, his gaze still focused on the tape on the bubble wrap. "Maybe I'll just . . . hang on to it." There were clearly more options than that. He just wasn't willing to share them. Yet.

After adding a dash of brandy and mini-marshmallows to each snowman mug, I returned to the table. "I'd love to see it." I was curious about the object that caused Sebastian to get so up in his own head.

He handed me the wrapped square and I took a seat, pulled away the tape, and unfolded the carefully wrapped packaging.

"It's very pretty," I said, setting down the mahogany box.

He hadn't looked at me since I'd found it. He'd done nothing but stare at the box. He leaned forward and lifted its lid and as he did, a familiar tune played. "My mother had one just like it. She kept her earrings in it."

"But she doesn't have it anymore?" I wasn't sure if he didn't want to talk about it or whether he was just caught up in his own thoughts.

"My father threw it across the room during one of their fights. I told you they used to fight a lot, right?"

"Yeah," I said, nodding. "It's why you didn't like Christmas as a kid."

"Right. Every time they were together, it was awful. I'd be just waiting for my dad to explode and my mother to shout back and then I'd sneak up to my bedroom and try to pretend it wasn't happening. They were terrible together. Christmas was worst because I expected more. Everyone said Christmas was a happy, joyful time. That's what I hoped for every year. And every year I was disappointed."

I was used to grumpy Sebastian, but never sad Sebastian. I wanted to scoop out the sorrow inside him and replace it with bright sunshine. Scooting forward in my chair, I threaded my fingers through the back of his hair. "Buying the box for her is so thoughtful of you."

He glanced up at me—the first time he'd looked at me since I'd discovered the music box. "Is it? Maybe she doesn't remember it. But it was one of the only times I ever saw her cry. The next thing I knew, they divorced. Maybe it would just bring long-forgotten wounds to the surface. If my father breaking the music box was the reason they divorced, then she won't want a constant reminder."

I shuffled my chair closer to him and leaned my head on his shoulder. "No one gets divorced over a music box. They get divorced because they're incompatible. That can show itself in lots and lots of different ways."

The music stopped.

He nodded but didn't say anything. He just picked up the box, turned it over, and wound up the mechanism at the bottom. The box began to play again. I couldn't bring to mind the name of the tune, only that it was familiar. It was a forlorn melody made a little sweeter because of the high, twinkly pitch.

"You think it's weird to replace something for someone all these years later, especially if it has such horrible memories attached to it?"

"I suppose you have to ask yourself why she was so upset when it was destroyed. It must have been very important to her. And I think if you, her son, were to give her another one after all these years, you've given her back a lovely memory. And it shows that you turned out to be a kind, thoughtful, good man. I think that's a wonderful association for that music box."

"Maybe," he said, still not convinced. "There's no rush anyway. It doesn't have to be this year that I give it to her. Probably best not to do it at Christmas anyway. She knows I don't celebrate and have so many bad memories of the season that it would probably taint the gift."

"Or wipe the slate clean," I suggested.

He didn't reply. We sat in silence for a few minutes until the music stopped again. Sebastian closed the lid and rewrapped the box and tucked it back in his pocket. The melancholy mood seemed to lift as soon as the trinket was out of sight.

"Is it wrong to toast with hot chocolate?" he asked, his mood brightening.

"Never, but especially not when there's brandy in it." I held up my cup.

"That's what I thought," he said, chinking his snowman mug to mine.

For a half-second, I allowed my mind to wander. Would Sebastian be here when my decorations came down? Would he help me put them up next year and then clink our hot chocolates at a job well done?

"What are you thinking?" he asked.

I smiled, pleased he cared but completely unwilling to answer. "What are you thinking?"

"I'm wondering whether or not your bedding is festive."

I slid off his lap and held out my hand. "You're in for a treat."

SEVENTEEN

Sebastian

If I'd been thinking clearly, I wouldn't be here tonight, but something drew me to Celia. Most men would have been attracted by her near-constant smile and her infectious, sunny energy. That, along with her perfectly round breasts and glossy, hip-length hair. But that wasn't *just* it for me. I was drawn to the bits of self-doubt she hid under the smile; the way when she spoke to someone, she focused all her attention on them as if they were the most important person she'd ever met; the almost too-blue eyes that told you exactly what she was feeling on the inside, no matter what her smile said. The curve of her back, the smooth skin of her neck, her delicate fingers and determined drive . . .

I really liked everything about her.

"Sebastian?" she asked, pulling me out of my thoughts. "Is it too much?" She glanced surreptitiously at her duvet cover, which boasted Christmas trees and snow-covered houses, and the fairy lights strung across her headboard.

I shook my head. That ex of hers had obviously done a

number on her. "I don't care what's on the bed, Celia," I said, pulling her toward me and lifting the hem of her pajama top, pushing it over her head. "I care who's in it." I dipped, placing a kiss on her collarbone and then on the other side of her bra strap, on her shoulder. Had there been any place I hadn't kissed her? There shouldn't be. I made a mental note to cover every part of her body from ankle to forehead with my lips.

She slid her arms around my neck and pressed her delicate fingertips into my skin.

"It's cold," she said with a shiver.

"Then I suggest we warm up." I slid her pajama bottoms over her hips and down her thighs. I held them as she stepped out, then placed a kiss on her stomach. I drank in the scent of fir and heat. I pulled out my wallet from my jeans, put it on the bedside table, and undressed as Celia watched, shifted her weight from one leg to another—in either cold or anticipation. Or both.

"I'm pleased you came over tonight," she said.

I took a step toward her and cupped the back of her neck in my hands. "I'm pleased too." I pressed my lips to hers and her tongue pushed between my lips. I couldn't help but groan at her determination. Her need.

I lifted her up and she wrapped her legs around my waist, but instead of heading to the bed, I turned and sat her on the chest of drawers opposite. It was the perfect height. And this way, I got to see her face-to-face while I drove into her.

"Here?" she asked, a little uncertain.

"Everywhere."

I pulled off her knickers and unsnapped the back of her bra. Cupping her breasts in my hands, I leaned forward, grazing each nipple with my teeth, breathing in her whimpers. I pressed my lips against the skin of her throat, trailed my tongue down between her breasts, over her stomach and down, her heat radiating into me and straight to my cock.

I paused, just above her clit. "You're fucking delicious."

She leaned back and pushed her tiny fingers into my hair, causing my erection to rear, as I pressed my tongue against her clit and through her folds, licking and sucking and pushing and pulling over and over and over until her body snapped and she shuddered around me.

I liked hearing her Christmas puns, despite my complaining. I liked talking to her and having her listen. But I *really* liked making her come.

"I thought I must have imagined how good this felt," she said, her voice whispery and light.

I shook my head, a growl of desperation gathering in my throat. "No. It's really this good." I grabbed a condom and pushed it over my tightening cock.

I took a breath, trying to relax, to push the stirrings at the base of my spine away, silence the thud of the blood in my veins.

I wanted this to last.

Sliding my crown over her gleaming wet pussy, I traced up and down her folds, coating my tip in her juices, trying to steady my heart rate before I pushed into her. It wasn't working.

"Sebastian," she whimpered, shifting.

"What?" I asked, touching my forehead to hers.

"I want you."

I bit down on my bottom lip and pushed into her as she gripped my shoulders. "Yes," she said, her voice soft but victorious as I pushed deep, deep, deep.

I lifted her knees and pushed deeper, grinding into her. She moaned my name like she'd never felt pleasure like it.

Pulling back, all I wanted to do was get as close as I could and I slammed back into her, making the dresser rock back and hit the wall. She gripped the edge of the wood and lifted her knees, urging me deeper still.

I slammed in again and again, blocking out everything but her heavy breaths on my neck, the grip of her fingers on my arms and the slide of her pussy.

I was so close so fast that I paused, trying not to focus on the soft, tight wetness surrounding my cock.

"You okay?" she asked. Her hand skidded up my sweat-sheeted back.

"More than okay. You're just so fucking perfect, Celia."

She pressed small kisses on my temple, my forehead, my cheek, and they brought me to life again. I began to move. Slow, lingering strokes, plowing deep into her.

I brought my forehead to hers, trying to control my breathing.

"It feels so good," she said. "Like you know exactly what I need."

That's how I felt—like somehow we were what each other needed, in bed and out of it. I groaned and pushed into her again, a little less controlled, a little more desperate to come, to make her come again.

She tipped her head back, exposing her smooth neck. I buried my face there, breathing her in, pushing hard and fast as if I were seconds away from victory in a marathon and only the scent of her was keeping me going.

She screamed my name, and convulsed underneath me. I let go, finally giving into the gnashing impatience of my climax. I pushed up and into her, half launching myself onto her.

The delicate press of her fingers stirred me back to consciousness.

"It's not enough," I said, half desperate, half delirious as I discarded the condom. "I just can't get enough of you."

She swept her hand over my bicep and wriggled off the chest. "Then take more," she whispered, a devil on my shoulder. She smoothed the back of her hand down my arm and placed my palm over her breast.

I groaned as I squeezed and pulled at her nipple. My cock reared back to life and I spun her around, facing the chest. One hand roamed over her breast and the other reached for her deliciously swollen clitoris. She reached around for her long plait and began to undo it as she squirmed under my fingers, hot against my chest.

She freed her hair and it fell like rain across our bodies. I pushed her forward. "Hold on," I choked out. I rolled on another condom and slammed straight into her, delighting at her gasp, driven half mad at the feel of her hair against my skin.

"Sebastian."

"I don't think I can ever stop," I said. I liked being with Celia. Liked watching her as she came up with a thousand ideas and ways of doing things. But fucking her? That was close to heaven.

"Don't," she bit out, dropping her head. "Ever."

My hand braced on her hip, we moved together like we'd been lovers for a lifetime. It was like she knew, some-how. Just a slight twist of her hips and her choking out my name. Or a clench of her pussy and a sexy, desperate glance over her shoulder. She understood everything I needed to rachet up my pleasure, knew what would have me fighting off my orgasm, trying to regain control.

I never did.

Instead, I inched relentlessly closer to another climax.

She arched her back, shuddering, and collapsed against

me, her legs shaking and her hands reaching for me. I kept fucking and fucking and fucking, desperate to make it last as long as possible just in case she disappeared back to wherever goddesses come from.

Just as I couldn't hold back another second, she pushed back hard and fast and I emptied myself into her.

I was still dizzy on the feel of her around my cock, still lightheaded at her softness in my hands and her sweet cries when she came, when she pushed away from me. And dropped to her knees.

She was just so fucking perfect. And it was *almost* too much.

Except it never would be.

I pulled off the condom and I didn't even feel the air hit my cock before her mouth was around my crown, licking and sucking, feeding on me like she'd been denied for a lifetime.

She pulled back. "I love your cock. Like maybe even more than Christmas."

I chuckled and threaded my hand through her hair. "I don't believe that for a second."

Her hot breath got me hard just when I would have put money on not being able have an erection again for a month because I was so spent. She took me so deep I almost came again as I hit the back of her throat. She pulled back, her teeth grazing my shaft. The sound of her wet tongue sent heat up my spine like lightning.

As she kneeled, head back, breasts high and firm, her hair streamed behind her like a waterfall pooling on the floor.

I cupped her head, enjoying the sight of her reddening lips as my cock pushed into her. She looked up at me, her eyes locking on mine. I wondered if I'd ever be able to look away.

Her hands on my thighs, she alternated between taking me oh-so-deep and working my crown like she was in my mind. I wasn't sure if it was her wet chin, her watering eyes, or her insistent tongue, but I was lost to this woman.

Completely and utterly lost.

I stepped away from her and lifted her to her feet, setting us both down on the bed. Again, I rolled a condom over my throbbing cock. I wanted her. I wanted to come inside her again, but I wanted her body meeting mine when I did.

I slid up into her and my entire body relaxed as we stroked and kissed and soothed each other. The frenzied fucking had passed and we moved languidly together, as if in some pre-rehearsed routine where each of us knew the steps. Within just a few minutes, I could tell that Celia was about to climax—not because she was scratching at me and screaming my name but because of the way her body tightened, almost imperceptibly; because of the way she looked at me, all openness and vulnerability.

We came at the same time, clutching at each other, sensation just as savage and uncontrollable as each time before, but somehow more focused and concentrated and most of all, shared between us.

She sighed as she pressed a kiss against my chest. "You're amazing." Her tone was dreamy and soft.

"You're everything." I'd never known anyone like her. Anyone so tough but soft. Anyone so desperate but determined. Anyone so fucking sexy. And kind. And passionate. And sweet.

And mine.

EIGHTEEN

Celia

I should be exhausted because it was so early. I knew I should sleep—we both should—but a warm, naked Sebastian was more than a little distracting. Far from being tired, I was now wide awake; my blood buzzed in my veins as my mind cycled through yesterday, last night, and what was going to happen today. I glanced at the clock on my bedside table. It was just gone six in the morning.

"You still have that bin bag of your ex's stuff?" Sebastian asked out of nowhere as we lay staring at the bedroom ceiling. I hadn't even realized he was awake.

"Yeah. I'll probably put it out for the bin men after Christmas." I would find the courage to do it sometime before next Christmas. I hoped. The more it sat under the kitchen table, the more significance the bag full of bric-a-brac took on. What was I trying to achieve by keeping it?

"Are you sleepy?"

"I wish I were sleepier," I replied.

"So, why don't we seize the moment?" he asked.

He can't have been talking about sex. If he was, he'd have been kissing me or pulling me onto him or . . .

"Let's go and make a fire in your garden and burn the contents of that bin bag."

He sat up and swung his legs off the bed, stretching up his arms as I appreciated the dip and curve of his muscular back in the glow of the bathroom light.

"Do you know how cold it is out there?" I asked. He was bonkers to even suggest it.

"We have coats," he said, padding into the bathroom. "And when the fire is going, it will keep us warm."

"I don't have materials for a fire." I wasn't sure what materials I'd need necessarily, but given I'd never made a bonfire in my back garden, I was confident I wouldn't have what we needed.

"You have matches. And paper. And a bag full of your ex-boyfriend's clothes and shit," he said, appearing in the doorway like he was about to be captured in marble by Michaelangelo.

"No thank you, I'm perfectly happy here in my warm bed."

"You know he's not coming back, right?"

I really didn't want to talk about this. I especially didn't want to talk about it with Sebastian. He didn't need to know that although I knew Carl wasn't coming back, there was a part of me that couldn't let go. "He might need those things," I said.

Instead of sliding back under the covers, Sebastian started pulling on his clothes. "If he needed anything in that bag, he would have been back by now."

He wasn't telling me anything I didn't already know.

"It's rude to just bin something of someone else's. I'm trying to take the high road."

He tried to tug the duvet off me but I held it tight. "No, it's rude to leave your girlfriend of six years on Christmas Eve without giving her any explanation. It's rude not to take all your stuff. It's rude not to treat you with the respect and dignity you deserve and it's just fucking senseless to leave you in the first place."

I exhaled, slightly exasperated. "I don't disagree with you about any of that. I just don't see how sending the village up in smoke is going to help."

"I'm not suggesting you take up arson as a hobby. He was a dick. Allocate him the responsibility he deserves, get angry about what he did, and then free yourself. Move on."

"You don't think I've moved on?" I raised my eyebrows, hoping he'd get my silent message that he was living proof I'd moved on plenty.

"I don't think anyone could move on while they hang on to a bunch of their ex's shit in a plastic bag. And don't give me that I've-moved-on-with-you bullshit. This isn't about whatever's going on with us. This is about you still thinking you need something from that man." This side of Sebastian where he was dominant and possessive and wanted more for me than I wanted for myself was part of him I could eat up with a spoon. It was like nothing and no one could stand in his way. "I've seen your fire when we're together. Harness it, let it rip and then refuel."

Somewhere in the last year, my brain had stopped *expecting* Carl to turn up wanting the rest of his things. But my heart had still been hoping for something. And now? It wasn't so much that I wanted him to come back, more that I wanted an explanation of why he left. That missing information was stopping me from closing the door and moving on.

"He should have told me he was leaving. He owed me

that. Something changed for him and I deserved to know what."

"Right," Sebastian said. "He was an arsehole."

"He was." There were no excuses to be made. He'd not behaved like the man I'd been with for the six years before.

"He's held you back while he's moved on."

Irritation pricked the back of my neck. God only knew what Carl was getting up to, and with who. I hadn't been able to even look at another man until nearly twelve months later, when Sebastian appeared in Snowsly. "I deserve better than Carl."

"You deserve a man who'll communicate to you how he's feeling. Not a boy who just runs away."

I sat bolt upright. "Exactly. Even if he left because he just didn't like me, he should have had the bollocks to say it to my face."

"Yes," Sebastian said.

"He never gave us a chance. He never had both feet in like I did. Because if he'd been committed to a future together, he wouldn't have left without warning—without some kind of indication he was unhappy."

I'd been so full of sadness about what I'd lost, I'd failed to look more closely at what had gone. I'd been grieving a lost future for the last twelve months without asking myself whether a future with a man like Carl was something that I really wanted. His leaving should have woken me up to the fact that Carl wasn't a man who deserved my heart. And he didn't deserve my grief, either. My future wasn't lost because he was gone. It was still mine to create.

I jumped out of bed and pulled on my clothes. "Yep. I'm ready." I popped the neck of my jumper over my head. "Let's burn his shit to the ground."

Sebastian grinned at me and pulled on his jumper.

"Actually, if I'm letting go of my past, then can you promise that you'll do the same? If I'm setting fire to Carl's stuff, can you promise you'll send your mother the music box for Christmas?"

He paused, his arm midair as his hand still searched for light through his sleeve. We locked eyes and I could see ten different ways he wanted to answer me in his expression. I knew Sebastian well enough now to know he wouldn't tell me he was going to do something if he didn't intend to follow through.

He finished pulling his jumper on and with a simple scrape of his fingers through his hair, Sebastian became catwalk ready. "I promise I'll consider it. With my mother, it's complicated."

"Okay, then that's a step forward at least. Let's get the matches."

As I emptied the bag out onto the small patio off the kitchen, I couldn't help but wonder why I'd been hanging on so tightly to this sorry pile of worn paperbacks and old clothes.

"It will all fit into the barbeque, I think." I scooped up the small mound of belongings and plonked them into the round metal barbeque that I never used.

Sebastian handed me the matches. "You want to say anything?"

"Like a spell or a hex or something?"

"Maybe? Or just something like goodbye. I don't know. I've not attended many burning rituals in my lifetime."

"Really?" I asked. "The way you advocated for this moment, I thought you were head of the Burning Rituals Lobby Group."

Sebastian smiled at me like he thought I was amazing.

When I was with him, I felt like I was. Or at least I could be.

I pulled out a match, lit it and tucked it under one of the pages of a worn, water-stained book. "Carl, you didn't deserve me. And I deserve to be rid of you." I lit another match and threw it on top of his AC/DC t-shirt and that bloody Star Wars duvet cover. "I don't want to waste another moment of my life thinking about you or your stupid t-shirts."

The fire began to burn harder now. More books were being eaten away by the fire and embers from the t-shirt had started to twist and curl.

Finally, I threw the Darth Vader pillowcase on top of the flames. Be gone, Vader.

NINETEEN

Sebastian

Everyone shifted in their seats in Granny's living room and began to stand as the morning Christmas Committee meeting at the Manor started to disperse.

Granny reached out and patted me on the hand. "Stay a minute, will you?"

As everyone filed out, Mary came in wheeling a tea trolley, Granny's favorite teapot and two cups set out on the top tray. "Biscuits are in the tin," she said, tapping the same purple-and-white-checked biscuit tin Granny had been using for the last thirty years.

"You pour the tea and I'll prize this thing open. I've got your favorites," Granny said, pulling the tin onto her lap.

"I have a favorite biscuit?" I couldn't remember the last time I'd eaten one. I poured out two cups of tea and added milk to both. I wasn't a big tea drinker but I'd had my first-ever cup with Granny. It was more about comfort than taste.

"Bourbons, of course,"

I nodded in recognition. I'd loved them as a boy. "Of course."

She offered me the open tin and I took out a chocolate Bourbon, getting the distinct impression I didn't really have a choice in the matter. Granny then took out a custard cream, because that had been her favorite biscuit for the last thirty years or more.

"It's wonderful news that takings have matched last year's," she said. Celia had nearly burst when Barbara announced the good news about turnover from yesterday, and I couldn't help but enjoy her excitement. Things were heading in the right direction. "I think it's a relief to everyone that Snowsville's market and my boo-boo with the website hasn't completely destroyed what we've built."

"I told you, you didn't do anything to the website. There was a technical issue." I wasn't going to tell anyone the website had been hacked. Tempers were frayed enough when it came to Snowsville. "The email to customers seemed to provide a boost, and hopefully the journalists visiting today and the changes we've made over the last couple of days, together with the branding, will mean profits grow for the rest of this year and into next year."

Granny shifted, lowering her foot to the floor, and picked up her cup. Seemed like she was getting better. "It's very good news. I knew you were going to be able to help. In a way, it's been good that I sprained my ankle." She winked at me.

Winked a you're-in-on-the-secret kind of wink.

"Granny." My tone was a warning. "*If* you sprained your ankle, then you need to keep it elevated," I reminded her.

"What do you mean *if*? You think I could have kept

myself away from that green over the last few days unless I was incapacitated?"

She might have a point.

"But now we're on the subject of you being here, how are you enjoying it?"

I didn't want to start comparing a private pool in Barbados with Snowsly's village green. "It's fine," I said.

"You think you might visit your old Granny a bit more often from now on?" A pang of regret bloomed in my chest until it was stopped in its tracks when she added, "I'm sure Celia would love to see you."

I shook my head, making no comment. Whatever I said, she'd manage to glean from it something I didn't mean.

But Granny wasn't deterred. "Her last boyfriend was just awful. Was about to propose to her and then just up and left. I never liked him one bit. Wasn't clever enough for Celia. I always think that women should marry someone smarter than they are. That way, they don't have to dim their light to preserve a man's ego. You, of course, can marry anyone in the country because you're the cleverest boy I know."

I chuckled. "I think you're slightly biased. And I'm pretty sure Celia wouldn't be able to dim her light even if she tried."

A grin unfurled on Granny's face as if she had me confessing to something I shouldn't have. But I'd played this particular game of chess with her before. "Exactly. I think that's why it ended. He couldn't keep up with her and didn't like to admit it. Anyway, I'm sure she'll find herself a nice young man before long. She's a beautiful girl."

I nodded, trying to ignore the not-so-subtle dance Granny was doing.

"I'm going to invite her over to the Manor for Christmas

lunch," Granny said. "There'll be quite the gathering. Most of the committee are coming. It would be nice to have you there."

I see, Granny. Checkmate. Her questions had been leading here all along. She wanted me to extend my stay. "You know I have a flight booked for Christmas Eve."

She sighed. "I do know that. I was just hoping you'd change your mind. I've waited so long to have you here at Christmas. Are you sure you can't wait a couple more days before you fly off?"

I'd always thought there wasn't anything I wouldn't do for Granny, but I might have just found my sticking point. The last few weeks had been more enjoyable than I could have expected. Better to leave when the going was good. The worst possible scenario would be ruining a perfectly lovely visit by overstaying. "You know I don't celebrate Christmas," I said. "You'll have much more fun without me."

She reached across and squeezed my hand. "How wrong you are, my darling boy. But I understand. The past is a painful place for you and understandably so for many reasons. But consider whether or not that's where you want to live."

"Have you spoken to Jocelyn?" I asked, wondering why she was bringing up the past.

She shook her head, her brow furrowed in disappointment. "Your mother calls me every week." It shouldn't surprise me that my mother called so often. She and Granny had always had a good relationship, which I found a little strange. Granny was so warm and loving and kind, and my mother had a hardness to her. She'd sent me to Snowsly every chance she got, after all. If I didn't know they were related, I would have thought their closeness impossible.

"Do you remember that jewelry box she had?" I asked. "It played a piece of music—I can't remember what it was called . . ."

"You don't remember?" Granny looked at me as if she thought I was joking.

"Why? Do you?"

"'Air,' by Henry Purcell. You used to play it on the piano as a child. You honestly don't remember?"

It had been a great number of years since my fingers had rested on piano keys. I'd given it up when I discovered girls.

"I bought that jewelry box for your mother precisely because I knew how proud she was when she listened to you play that piece of music."

Confusion hit me in the chest like a bag of hammers. It was as if someone had pulled not just the rug, but the entire floor from underneath me. "She loved that music box."

"She certainly did." She sucked in a breath. "She was devastated when it was destroyed." Throughout my parent's acrimonious divorce, Granny never spoke a single word against my father. The expression on her face now was as close as she'd come to criticism.

"I never knew." I'd always known my mother had been upset about the music box, but I hadn't ever understood why. It certainly hadn't occurred to me it was because she'd lost something sentimental that involved *me*. I'd always seen her frustrated or angry.

"It killed her to send you to me so often. She'd miss you so much, but she wanted to protect you from their fighting."

She sent me to Snowsly to protect me? That was news to me. I suppose I hadn't really thought about why she'd done it—I was too busy being grateful that she'd sent me here.

"She wanted to protect me?"

"Of course. She knew it wasn't healthy for you to grow up with her and your father always arguing. And while she found her strength to leave him, she wanted you to be in a place you could be a child and have fun."

So it wasn't that she hadn't wanted me, more that she'd wanted *more* for me.

"The music box was a part of you that she could keep when you were away," Granny said. "And then when it broke . . ."

She was devastated. I knew that. I'd seen it. I just hadn't known why. Sadness trickled through my body. Why hadn't anyone told me before what that music box meant? Why hadn't I understood that the reason I was sent away from my parents was to protect me, not because they didn't want me.

"Why didn't she or you or anyone explain?" I asked, irritation rising in my gut.

Granny laughed. "Sebastian Fox! Me and your mother have both tried to talk to you about those years countless times before. No one can tell you anything you don't want to hear. I'm glad that seems to have changed."

Exhaling, I tried to recall either of them saying anything about the divorce. I couldn't bring anything specific to mind but they were right—I didn't like to discuss what went before. I didn't want to talk about the past because I didn't want to remember what it was like to live it.

If I hadn't heard that music box, I would have never have known any of this. And if I hadn't just been discussing it with Celia, I wouldn't have brought it up with Granny. I might never have found out why my mother had been so upset to lose that music box.

I might never have known how treasured I'd been as a child. How much love might still be waiting for me, if only I'd let go of the past and grab hold of it.

I finished up my tea and set down my cup. "Thanks for the chat, Granny." I stood and kissed her on her head. "I'm off to greet the journalists. I'll let you know how it goes." I had a stop to make before I led a tour around the market. I'd have just enough time.

She patted me on the cheek like she'd been doing my entire life. "Make sure you introduce Celia. They're bound to feel her infectious joy and translate that into their articles. No one can help but fall in love with her enthusiasm."

I ignored her comment and headed to the door.

TWENTY

Sebastian

As I wandered up to the green, I glanced up at a helicopter overhead that had everyone working the Snowsly Christmas market staring into the sky. In a few seconds, it disappeared. It must have landed.

Celia was in front of me, her phone in the air, video calling someone. "Isn't it pretty?" she asked.

"Who's that behind you?" whoever was on the phone asked. Celia snapped her head around, her grin widening when she saw me. There was something about the woman that meant I couldn't not smile when she was around. What had she done to me?

"That's Sebastian," she said.

I dipped my head. "Hi, whoever you are."

"I'm Lemon," she replied. "It sounds like you've saved Christmas this year."

"Nice to meet you—I've heard only good things. But if you're really Celia's best friend, you know that can't possibly be true. We make a good team—a team led by Celia."

Celia and I locked eyes and she scrunched up her nose as if I'd given her a false compliment. If only she saw how capable she was.

"Oh, aren't you just charming." Celia pulled down her phone, presumably in case her friend said too much. "I hope you're around next year because I'm coming to the UK to experience my first Snowsly Christmas," her friend called from where she was facing Celia's coat.

"Gotta go," Celia said and cancelled the call. "She wanted to come this year but she's in New York. I think I told you. Anyway, I'm sure you think that's no big deal because, you know, Christmas is no big deal to you, but I hate that she's not here. I want everyone who's important to me around me at Christmas."

"That makes sense," I said. People mattered. Perfection didn't. "Take lots of photos to send her because the village looks amazing—like something you'd see on a Christmas jigsaw puzzle."

"It always does. I think we're all prepared," she continued. "Howard's going to collect the journalists from the station. All the stallholders have restocked and all the decorations have been checked. We're ready for anything." She winced. "I shouldn't have said that. With our luck, the green will burn to the ground before it's dark."

I laughed. "There will be no fires. I won't allow it."

A group of people on the other side of the green started shouting and waving. "Sebastian," I heard someone call.

I squinted at the group of people barreling toward me. "Griffin!" I'd told him what I was up to and asked him to rustle up some social media influencers. He'd never let me down before. I just hadn't expected he'd bring them himself. By helicopter.

"I wanted to see the place that pulled you away from the Caribbean." He took my arm and gave me a half hand shake, half hug.

"You were in the helicopter?" Of course he was. I don't know why I bothered to ask.

"Gotta get my use out of it. And it only took us thirty minutes from London. There's so much space out here." *Spot the Londoner who never leaves the city.*

"Very different from Mayfair," I said. Griffin usually liked London. And sun-soaked beaches. And nothing in between.

"Celia, this is Griffin. Griffin, Celia. Griffin's my oldest friend," I explained. "Who's apparently flown from London to experience Snowsly's Christmas Market."

"There's no better place at Christmas," Celia said, her eyes reflecting the lights of the Christmas tree at the center of the green.

"Good to meet you, Celia." Griffin glanced at me, then at Celia, then back at me. I could tell he was having a conversation with himself, noting how attractive Celia was, speculating as to whether there was anything between us. He was undoubtedly wondering if she found him attractive.

He was nothing if not predictable.

"You've been having fun," Griffin said. He winked at me, having worked out my bond with Celia. We'd known each other a long time.

"Oh, and I brought one or two friends," Griffin said, his hand waving in the direction of the other four members of his group. "You said you were trying to get some social media coverage. These guys are . . . you know. They're on Instagram."

A smile unfurled on my face. Griffin was a master of the understatement. "They're on Instagram?"

"And one's on TikTok, whatever the hell that is. But they love this kind of thing. Figured I might as well fill the helicopter."

I punched Griffin on the arm. "Thank you."

"Nothing to thank me for. I'm here to do my Christmas shopping. It's busy," he said, surveying the green, "but not as bad as bloody Bond Street this time of year." He turned, waved his hand in the air, and headed to the first stall.

"Well, if he gets his credit card out, we can about guarantee Snowsly will have their best year ever. He makes me look like I'm living paycheck to paycheck." Griffin might just be the richest man in England. But what I liked about him is that he underplayed everything—his wealth, his loyalty, and his kindness.

"How do you know him?"

I turned to Celia. "Funny story. I met him on Christmas Day, on a beach in the northern part of Western Australia. We were both eighteen and away from home. Haven't been able to get rid of him since."

"You don't mean that."

I smiled. Celia always believed the best about everyone. I wondered for a second what that would be like. "No, I don't. Speaking of exaggerations, I can guarantee you when Griffin says the people he's brought 'have Instagram,' they're some of the most powerful influencers in the British Isles."

Celia bounced on her toes, though whether she was excited or trying to keep warm, I couldn't quite tell. "So, barring flood or fire, it looks like we're all set to have a great rest of the season."

I glanced up at the sky as snow began to fall. "It's not

looking like rain. Let's just keep our fingers crossed about the fire."

I grabbed her hand, threading my fingers through hers as she grinned up at me. Yes, the tree looked festive and the market stalls had their lights perfectly positioned. But there was nothing more beautiful than seeing Celia happy.

TWENTY-ONE

Sebastian

It didn't matter that I thought this was a terrible idea. Granny was determined.

"It's a sprained ankle and I've been off it for almost two weeks. I'm going stir crazy at the Manor." Sitting in the wheelchair, wrapped up in nine layers, she waved her walking stick in front of her like I needed directions to the village green. "I'm going to put the Snowsly bauble on the tree if it's the last thing I do."

The swelling around her ankle seemed to have subsided, so I'd relented and agreed to take her out. It was coming up to five and the sky was almost black, but even from the top of the hill, the sparkling lights of the Snowsly Christmas Market were visible.

"I want to see all the signs up, and these picture stations that you lot keep talking about."

"I've shown you photographs," I said. "Anyway, we'll pass them on our way. I'm not sure why you're still complaining."

"Because I'm getting old and that's what old people do. We complain." She laughed at herself and tucked her tartan blanket over her legs.

"You'll never be old to me," I said. I didn't want to think about Granny getting old. She had so much energy and spirit, she'd probably live to two hundred.

"Finally, I have an *excuse* to complain. Don't spoil it for me."

As we got to the edge of the green, Granny sighed contentedly. I paused the wheelchair so she could take in the scene: Snowsly's Christmas tree stood tall and proud in the center; the German market stalls covered in lights circling the tree. The market was full of people, wrapped up in hats and gloves and scarfs, still smiling and laughing despite the frost in the air. The new Snowsly Christmas Market sign was lit up at the entrance to the market. Christmas music played from the speakers dotted through the market, and the scent of roasting chestnuts and hot chocolate wound its way down to us.

"Sebastian, it's everything I hoped it would be. It's beautiful." She reached back and took my hand.

"It's very pretty," I said, squeezing back. "Festive. You should be very proud."

"I'm proud of *you*. Thank you for coming. It's meant so much to me." Her voice faltered.

"Hey," I said. "I don't think the market was in any danger of being a disaster. Celia would have fixed things."

Two weeks ago, the idea that I'd actually enjoy being in the middle of nowhere, immersed in everything Christmassy, was ridiculous. But these last two weeks had been far from the torture I'd expected. Snowsly felt like home even though I'd not been here for so long. Seeing Granny in her own surroundings made me appreciate how important this time had been. Like it or not, she was getting older. And maybe she needed me now, just like I'd needed her so many years ago. I also found I loved the space of the country—the mist in the morning and the mooing of the cows. I'd enjoyed not being in London.

"I know," she said, releasing my hand. "We would have gotten by without you. It's just been nice not to have to. That's all."

My heart squeezed in my chest and I started the wheelchair toward the green. Howard saw us and waved.

"Good to see you out and about, Ivy." He offered to take the wheelchair from me and I let him. "Can I get you some hot chocolate?"

I glanced down the rows of stalls. In the crowds, I spotted a flash of white-blonde hair and my insides warmed. Celia was beautiful. Kind. Creative. Caring.

"Ivy!" Celia said as she approached us, red baubles apparently sewn onto her coat back and front. "It's so good to see you up here. Have you got the Snowsly bauble?"

She tapped the box on her lap. "All ready to be placed on the tree. Better late than never, right?"

Howard handed Granny her hot chocolate and she took a sip. "Gorgeous, Howard. But I like a little brandy in mine."

I locked eyes with Celia and she let out a laugh. "Me too, Ivy," she said.

"Let's go put up this bauble," Granny said.

On our way to the tree, we stopped by a picture station featuring a seven-foot nutcracker in his green, red, and white uniform. This one and the others—a classic Frosty complete with cob pipe, and a beautifully decorated white Christmas tree—had Snowsly Christmas signs in front, so no one was in any doubt where the people in the photographs were having a wonderful time.

"Wait for me," Keely called as she joined our group.

As we got to the base of the tree, the Christmas music faded and Jim's voice came through the speakers. "Join us over at the tree as our own Ivy Fox hangs the ceremonial Snowsly Christmas bauble on the tree. Replica baubles are available to purchase from every stall in the market." Then the Christmas music resumed.

"I suppose that's my cue," Granny said. She opened the box on her lap and pulled out the large clear snowflake, *Wishing You a Very Snowsly Christmas* etched into the surface.

Celia clasped her hands together. "I'm so pleased you managed to make it out. It looks beautiful, Ivy."

"Thanks to you, Celia, my dear. You're a very special girl." Granny glanced at me, just to make sure I knew Celia had her seal of approval. Of course, I already knew. As much as I'd enjoyed every second of her company, I was leaving tomorrow.

Celia belonged here in Snowsly.

Granny placed the bauble on the tree. I wheeled her back a meter or so, to see how it looked.

"Beautiful," she declared.

A piercing scream toward the Christmas shop stall took our attention. A corner of the market had been plunged into darkness. All the lights had gone out on three stalls.

"I knew it," Celia said, starting toward the commotion.

"Granny, are you okay here if I go and—"

"Get over there," she said, shooing me away. "Howard and Keely will look after me."

I ran after Celia, through the crowds of people, sending up a prayer than no one had been hurt. The Snowsly

Christmas market had been a phoenix rising from the flames. I just hoped those flames weren't about to burn us to the ground.

I caught up to Celia and arrived at the Christmas Shop stall at the same time.

"What happened?" Celia asked breathlessly.

"I don't know," Barbara said. "The lights just went out."

"It must be the generator," Celia said. "It powers these three stalls." She scrambled behind the stall and I followed her. "Yep. It's stopped running." She glanced at me, a mixture of disappointment and fury pooling in her eyes. "I can't believe it. It's the twenty-third of December. There's no way I'm going to be able to find a new one."

"What about Mr. Taylor in Snowsville?" Barbara suggested. "He might be able to fix it."

"Snowsville? No one there is going to help us," Celia said. "These were the people who took down our tree."

"We don't know that," I said, putting my hand on Celia's shoulder.

"Wait!" said Celia, leaning over. I couldn't see what she was fiddling with. Just as I was about to pull her off so she didn't get hurt, the lights came back on.

Celia turned and grinned. "They'd just come unplugged."

I laughed, watching her bright, ice-blue eyes sparkle. "You're amazing."

"It was a plug. Even I can deal with unplugged lights."

And a whole lot more.

TWENTY-TWO

Celia

Since we'd gotten stuck in Snowsville, every evening Sebastian would either walk me home or appear at my door at some point after I'd gotten into my pajamas. We'd spend the rest of the night together, swapping stories, drinking hot chocolate or just straight brandy, and then exploring each other's bodies like we knew time was running out.

Tonight was the twenty-third. Our last night together.

Although not unexpected, when he knocked on the door, my stomach dived to the floor as if tonight was somehow different. Maybe because I was hoping that he'd tell me he'd decided to stay for Christmas. Or even move here.

A part of me, a completely unrealistic, Santa-believing part of me was hoping this wasn't going to be our last night together.

"Should I ask about the wand?" He nodded toward the pink glitter wand in my hand. "You know this is Christmas and not wizard school, right?"

"Semantics. It's all magic."

He smiled and shook his head in a way I'd come to recognize as saying, *I'm-not-quite-sure-what-to-do-with-you-but-I'm-rolling-with-it*. Much better than the disdainful look I'd come to expect from Carl when I was involved with anything Christmassy. Or frankly did anything that I enjoyed. Looking back, I don't think he liked me that much. It can't have always been like that. We must have had some good times. It was difficult to remember them now.

"You want a drink?"

"You're not wearing Christmas pajamas. What's going on?" He unbuttoned his coat and pulled out a padded envelope.

I shrugged. "I've only just got in." I glanced at the bag. "What's this?"

Sebastian took a seat at his usual sky-blue chair at the kitchen table while I set the bag next to him before pulling out mugs for our drinks. "Open it," he said. "Before you make drinks."

I glanced over at him, trying to get a read on his expression. If I didn't know better, I would say it was slightly bashful. "Is it a gift?" I asked as I peered into the bag.

He replied with a shrug. "I'm not a great wrapper."

"But I've already had a beautiful Secret Santa gift from you." I kept the weather house in my bedroom so I could see it as soon as I woke up and last thing before I went to sleep.

"This isn't from Secret Santa. It's from me. Just open it, but don't get excited. It's very practical."

I tried my best not to break into a grin but it was supremely difficult, given the handsome reformed grinch had bought me a *second* Christmas present. He might be leaving tomorrow, but tonight he was making me feel like I was at the center of his world.

I shook my head, trying to push silly thoughts like that out of my brain. I wasn't the center of Sebastian's world. Tomorrow he was leaving, and the practical part of me doubted I'd ever see him again.

I pulled a slim parcel from the bag. "What is it?" I asked, shaking it.

"I know it's a radical idea, but why don't you get it out and have a look?"

I tore the wrapping paper off to reveal a padded envelope. Inside were a set of keys. I glanced across at Sebastian. What had he bought?

"You want to take a look?"

"Keys to what?"

He pulled them out of my hand, stood and ushered me to the front door.

He grabbed the blue and white bobble hat I'd worn to the Snowsville Christmas market and plonked it on my head, so low I had to push it up to see.

Then he opened the door.

"Ivy tells me people fill each other's stockings with practical gifts," he said. "I couldn't find a stocking big enough, but I think this fits the brief." He stepped aside to reveal a bright red Mini.

It was as if someone had thrown a snowball at me and it had landed square in my chest, knocking out my breath.

"You'd be better off with a Land Rover around here, but I didn't think it would particularly suit you," he said. "So I chose a Mini. With four-wheel drive."

I knew I should say something, but what? "You . . . bought me a car?"

"You need one," he said, like he'd just bought me a colander. "I don't know how your petrol tank suddenly emptied itself, but a car that's doing stuff like that isn't safe."

He wasn't wrong, but a car? "So you fixed it. Like the web site and branding and the tree . . . bringing influencers and journalists to the market. You like to fix things."

"Are you upset?" he glanced at me and pushed his hands into his pockets.

I was being rude. "Of course not." I reached for him, wrapping my arms around his waist. "It's just . . . No one's ever bought me a car before. I'm a little lost for words. But completely in a good way. Thank you. It's incredibly generous of you. Are you sure?"

He pressed a kiss to the top of my head as we stood gazing at the brand-new Mini. "Of course I'm sure. Just one condition, I don't want you to drive it for the first time in the dark. Can you wait until tomorrow?"

He was so caring and protective. I would never have guessed it when I'd first met him. But if he cared enough to buy me a car and worry about my safety, couldn't he care enough to stay? I knew it was hopeless, but I couldn't help but wish. "If I didn't know you were so determined to leave, I might try to convince you to stay."

He pulled me tighter. "I can't."

"Not even just for Christmas? I heard Barbados is beautiful in January."

"The last two weeks have been . . . great. Much . . . better than I expected."

I rolled my eyes. Here was the grinch back. "Well, on behalf of Snowsly, we're pleased it hasn't been so much of an endurance for you to be back. And we'll see you in another ten years." As soon as I'd said the words, I wished I could take them back, or at least re-say them without the snappish tone. I didn't want to ruin anything. I just didn't want him to leave.

A twitch at the corner of Sebastian's eye hinted that we

were veering into uncomfortable territory. "You're a great person, Celia."

My stomach churned at his words and I shook my head. "We don't need to have this conversation. It was a joke that came out wrong. I know this was never anything more than a . . . pre-Christmas fling. And it's been lovely." My voice had reached ridiculously high notes. "I don't want to spoil it."

"I'll be up more often now. Granny's getting older and it's selfish to expect her to come to London. And Griffin being here in thirty minutes in his helicopter—well, I'd never considered that I could cut out the drive like that. I'll be around, but—"

"I never had any expectations and I'm not asking for anything." I really wasn't but at the same time, if he'd turned around to me and said, *I've really enjoyed this and I really like you and I'd like to see how things go, and what if you come up to London and I can come up to Snowsly*—urgh how was I holding out hope for something so completely unrealistic?

I hadn't even let my brain dare think about these things before now. It was always completely clear that whatever was between us would be fleeting and short-lived. That had always been fine—better, even, because I didn't have to think about anything but him when we were together. Not the future, not the past. Only now I couldn't help but think about all the what-ifs. All the maybes. All these things he could have said but hadn't.

I'd never really expected that he would.

It just would have been nice to spend this Christmas with a man as good and decent as Sebastian. The more I thought about it, the more I realized that the past few weeks with Sebastian had been more fun than all the years I'd spent with Carl. I liked Sebastian, so much. And I thought he liked me. It seemed such a wasted chance.

"Promise me one thing," I said.

"Name it," he said, pulling away a little so I could look him in the eye.

"Don't come and find me before you leave tomorrow. I don't like Christmas Eve goodbyes."

He swept my hair behind my ear and placed a kiss at the corner of my mouth.

"I promise I'll just disappear."

I didn't want to trigger any memories about last year and coming home to Carl packing. Not that Carl and Sebastian were similar in any ways that counted. I just wanted to remember my time with Sebastian as it had been—carefree and happy and unburdened by histories or futures.

If being with Sebastian meant I had to give him back, it was a price I was willing to pay.

TWENTY-THREE

Sebastian

The final night of the Christmas market was in full swing, which meant it was time for me to leave. Despite protestations from Mary, I carried my own suitcase from my room to my car and handed it to Bradley.

I'd already said my goodbyes to Granny and told her I'd be back to see her after Christmas. I had to leave now to be sure of not missing my flight.

"Good to have you here," Mary said from the entrance of the Manor. "Don't leave it so long next time."

I kissed her cheek. "Thank you for taking such good care of Granny. Make sure she does the exercises the physio gave her." I don't know why I bothered to say anything. Mary wouldn't let Granny get away with anything when it came to her recovery.

I opened the passenger side of the car and dipped my head to climb in.

"Sebastian!" a voice from the dark called. Even though I could tell from the tone that it wasn't Celia, for a second before logic took over, I thought it could be. And my stomach flipped at the thought.

Just a final kiss. A final touch. A goodbye.

"Barbara," I said as she scurried toward me as fast as the icy ground would allow.

"Just a little something for the journey," she said, handing me a plastic bag.

I peered in.

"Shortbread," she explained. "And a Chocolate Orange."

Memories of Barbara from when I was a boy flooded in. She'd always been so kind to me. Let me play with the decorations in the Christmas shop. Stopped by the Manor every day the summer I got chicken pox, bringing DVDs and ice lollies. I'd forgotten so much.

"I haven't had a Chocolate Orange in years."

Barbara beamed at me. "You used to love it when I saved you some for when you'd visit after Christmas."

I nodded, remembering the scrunched-up orange foil containing three or four slices of chocolate that Barbara would press into my hand and tell me not to tell Granny about. I would always tell Granny—better that than she find out of her own accord. But she'd always let me keep the gifted chocolate.

"Thank you. I'll enjoy that on my trip."

"Oh and this," she said, holding out a giftwrapped square. "Celia asked me to pass it along." She covered her mouth. "I shouldn't have given it away." She shook her head, chastising herself. "Well, you know now. She was your Secret Santa."

I forced a smile. "Thank her for me, will you?"

Barbara fixed me with a look that said she really wanted

to tell me to thank Celia myself. But she nodded and patted my hand. "Don't be a stranger."

"I promise I'll be back soon."

I kissed her on the cheek then slid into the passenger seat. Bradley pulled away, leaving the Manor, the green, and a lot of memories, old and new, in the rearview mirror.

As we wound through the village, I turned over the wrapped present from Celia. George Michael was finally singing "Last Christmas" in the front. The music stopped abruptly.

I snapped my head up.

"Sorry, Sebastian," Bradley said. "It's on the radio. Shall I try to find something less festive, or would you prefer silence?"

"It's fine," I said. "You can turn it back on." It was the one Christmas song I'd not heard this year. Anyone would think Snowsly had put a ban on it or something.

I caught his frown of confusion in the mirror. I'd been unable to enforce it in the office but "no Christmas music" had always been a strict rule in the car. After the last fortnight, I wouldn't say I enjoyed Christmas music exactly, but I wouldn't say I didn't enjoy it either. After all, it reminded me of the last two weeks. And those two weeks were everything I could have hoped for from Snowsly. And more. None of the regret at having missed all those Christmases as a child had risen to the surface. None of the dashed hope had emerged. I'd just had a really good time.

I pulled at the wrapping on the gift, only then realizing there were actually two gifts held together with the ribbon. I grinned to myself, almost excited to see what she'd bought.

Before I could tear into the paper, my phone buzzed.

It was my mother. She never called.

I accepted the call and braced myself for bad news.

"Hello, mother."

"Sebastian," she said, her voice soft and floaty.

"Is everything okay?"

She pulled in a breath on the other end of the phone. "I received your gift today and . . ."

I never bought my mother Christmas gifts. Ever. Not since I was a child. She probably felt awkward at having to acknowledge it. "I just saw it and thought you might like it. It's no big deal," I said, keen to sweep any awkwardness away.

"It's wonderful." Her voice broke as she spoke and a bolt of shock passed down my spine. She was . . . happy?

She cleared her throat. "I can't believe you remembered the box. It was broken so long ago."

I pulled in a breath, determined to be honest with her. There had been too many unspoken words between us. "It was the only time I'd ever seen you cry."

"Yes, I was very upset. I would play it last thing at night before I went to sleep. It reminded me of you when you were with Granny."

The way she said it proved to me that what Granny had revealed was true. My mother had missed me. She hadn't sent me to Granny's because she didn't want me around, but because she'd wanted me to be happy. She'd wanted me to have the childhood she remembered.

"Granny said I used to play the tune on the piano."

She laughed. "Over and over and over. But I loved it. And I missed it when you were gone. I missed you. And when it broke, it was like I'd lost you completely. It may seem like just a music box but it's so much more. And now you giving me this one—it's almost exactly the same—and at Christmas . . . It's made this Christmas into the best Christmas ever, Sebastian."

I grunted. "Well, it's a low bar."

Both of us were silent for a few beats.

"I never understood why you stopped celebrating after your gap year. Growing up in Snowsly, I'd always loved Christmas so much. I wanted to pass that joy down to you, but somehow I managed to do the opposite. Was it because you didn't like the commerciality of it, or was it too childish?"

Did she really not know?

"You and dad were always arguing," I said.

"But not at Christmas. Even after the divorce, we had an agreement that we never argued over Christmas. We had a very strict rule. And that's why I always felt okay keeping you home for the festive season."

Was she high or was I losing it? Our memories were diametrically opposed. I thought back to those Christmases. The terse words while we opened stockings. The way they'd try not to look at each other while they discussed what Christmas film we were going to watch. The three of us around the dining table wearing paper hats, while my mum and dad tried not to let their pasted-on smiles slip. My jaw clenched and my shoulders inched higher just thinking about those times.

Maybe they hadn't been arguing, but because they'd been trying so hard not to, it just felt like they may as well have been at each other's throats.

"I hate to tell you mum, but the tension could be sliced with a spoon. I swear, I developed gray hairs spending Christmas with you and dad."

"Really? I'm so sorry. I tried so hard to make it special. Is that why you don't celebrate?"

"Partly," I said, only partly telling her the truth. Unbeknownst to me, she'd obviously been trying to create the

Snowsly Christmas magic. She'd had good intentions. I didn't need to devastate her by telling her that every year, I'd listened to her talk excitedly about Christmas and every year, I thought things would be different. That Christmas would be just as magical as she had described. And every year, my stomach churned with tar at the reality of the situation.

"How come we never went to Snowsly for Christmas if you loved it so much as a child?"

"Your father hated being out of the city. You know what he was like."

That made sense. He'd been a creature of habit. Liked his routine and home comforts.

"And I didn't want to deny him a Christmas with his son."

I glanced out of the window at the dark hedgerows. How sad that two people who wanted their son to be happy, managed to achieve the exact opposite.

"What about now? You never come over to Snowsly at Christmas now."

"Granny's busy. And you're not there. It feels like it wouldn't be the same as I remembered. I'd rather keep the great memories as wonderful as they are and not ruin them."

My heart squeezed in my chest.

"Snowsly is still a very special place at Christmas," I said, a reel of memories of the last few weeks whirring through my brain. "I've been helping Granny with the market. It's really quite . . ." *Magical* was the word that sprung to mind, but I didn't believe in magic. Despite the disasters that had seemed to strike on an almost-daily basis, we kept our spirits up and, in the end, the market and the village were better for surviving them. Everyone pulled together and created a Christmas team—a family—that could be counted on in any situation.

She sighed. "Yeah, she said you'd been. That's very good of you to change your holiday plans. You know what?" she asked, her tone brightening, but still melancholy underneath. "I'm going to imagine myself back at Snowsly this year."

She sounded so low. So sad. I wasn't sure if she never sounded like this or if I'd just never heard it—tuned it out somehow. Like I'd learned to tune out their fighting. My brain started to jog into gear, then broke into a sprint.

"I've got an idea," I said. "A proposition, if you like."

"Tell me," she replied.

I couldn't believe I was about to suggest what I was going to say. But Granny was getting older and I wasn't a child anymore. And I'd had a damn good time the last few weeks. I didn't need to lie to convince my mother that Snowsly was still a magical place—because it *was* still a magical place. And if that was the case, why was I heading to Barbados for Christmas?

Why in the hell wasn't I spending Christmas with my family? My Snowsly family.

"Why don't we both go to Snowsly for Christmas next year?"

I thought I heard a half-sob on the other end of the phone. "There's nothing I'd love more than to spend Christmas with you again, Sebastian. Being in Snowsly would be the icing on the cake."

"The Christmas cake," I added and she let out a half-laugh. "It was good to talk to you, mum."

"And you, my darling son."

"I'll call you tomorrow to wish you a Happy Christmas."

We said our goodbyes and I hung up, feeling like a life-time's worth of unspoken truths had finally been said and a childhood of acrimony had melted away.

I felt lighter. Happier. And I felt bloody festive. Spending next year in the UK for Christmas didn't seem so daunting. What did I have to lose? I knew I'd let go of the lost Christmases I'd never experienced as a child. I wasn't a child anymore. If it turned out to be terrible, it wasn't the end of the world. But the last weeks had shown me that Snowsly in the run-up to Christmas was anything but terri-ble. It was full of warmth and kindness and people looking out for each other. There was nothing to suggest that was all going to dry up as soon as the clock struck midnight on Christmas Eve. Next year, I'd spend Christmas in Snowsly and finally get the Christmas I'd always wanted as a child. Hopefully, Granny would be thrilled.

I turned back to unwrapping the present Celia had bought me. The first one was square and hard and felt a lot like a book. I ripped back the paper to reveal a copy of *The Night Before Christmas*.

I opened the cover and inside was an inscription.

Even if you don't like Christmas, I know for sure you like what comes before.

She was right. I'd enjoyed all the buildup. The happi-ness on people's faces as they shopped in the market. The lights that seemed to make the dark something to crave. And the hot chocolate—with or without brandy. I'd even started to enjoy the dulcet tones of Michael bloody Bublé.

I set the book to one side and opened the second gift. It was a framed photograph of Snowsly, obviously taken in the last few days. The Manor stood tall and proud in the back-ground, while in the foreground, Celia had managed to capture the delight and activity of the Christmas market. I turned it over as if searching for more. And I found it. On the back, she'd written, *To keep you company on Christmas Day. Wish you were here.*

A deep sense of belonging settled low in my chest. What was I doing? What was I running from? If I was prepared to risk Christmas in Snowsly next year, then why not now?

"Bradley?"

Our eyes met briefly in the rear view. "Yes?"

"Please turn the car around and head back to Snowsly. I'm going to be spending Christmas in the Cotswolds."

TWENTY-FOUR

Celia

There was only one explanation for me hiding behind a bush, two hot chocolates in hand. It was dark, freezing cold, and my thighs burned because of the half-squat I'd forced myself into. I dipped my head as I silently chastised myself for wearing my bright red Christmas hat. At least I'd turned off the flashing lights of my favorite Christmas cardigan.

The simple explanation for my Twister-inspired pose was that I just couldn't say goodbye to Sebastian. I had my reasons. I didn't want to embarrass myself and tell Sebastian how much I wanted him to stay. I didn't want to let the tears that were gathering in the corners of my eyes overspill. And I didn't want to ruin my Christmas. I was still determined that everything was going to be perfect. Even if I was alone.

As Sebastian's car faded away into the dark corridors of the winter roads, I straightened and headed towards the Manor.

"You've just missed Sebastian," Barbara said. At least

I'd been successful in hiding. "But I gave him the gift you left."

I smiled as genuinely as I could muster. "Thanks, Barbara. He'll be in Barbados soon."

"I can't understand it," she said. "Who'd want to be anywhere but here?" She glanced over at the green below us.

"Not all those people spending money, that's for sure."

With the coverage on the *Good Housekeeping* and *Rallegra* social media, together with the Instagram influencer attention we'd been getting, business had never been so good. I'd set up some social media accounts for the village and we already had over a hundred thousand followers. People came from far and wide to visit and take pictures and drink hot chocolate.

And it wasn't just footfall. The visitors had come with money in their pockets and we were on track to have our most successful Christmas season ever, despite the slow start.

We'd done it. We'd saved Christmas.

"Just going to pop in and give Ivy this hot chocolate," I said to Barbara as I stepped over the threshold of the Manor. "Catch up later."

Maybe Ivy's sprained ankle had been far from the disaster I'd first thought it was. After all, it had brought Sebastian to the village. He'd brought his new ideas and sometimes his brute strength. And he'd brought lazy hours spent around my kitchen table, and scorching hot nights in bed.

Sebastian had made Christmas for me this year, even if he didn't stay for the day itself. I was so sad he'd gone.

But he had. And I'd survive. Better that he go now so I didn't have longer to get to like him even more.

As I reached the back sitting room, I found Ivy, without a Zimmer frame, walking around the room. "Ivy! Aren't you supposed to be resting?"

She nearly hit the ceiling as if she'd been caught stealing from the till. "I'm just doing as I'm told. You know me. The physio said I need to start walking again. And actually, there's less pain than I expected."

"That's great. I brought you some hot chocolate." I set it down next to her seat on the sofa. "I'm just leaving it here."

"Did you catch Sebastian? He just left."

I shrugged, trying to come across as blasé. "Must have just missed him. He get off okay?"

Ivy hobbled back and sank into the sofa. I took a seat on the wingback chair next to her. "I suppose." She pushed her lips together and shook her head like she was trying to solve a puzzle. "I really thought he'd stay. I'd been hoping at least."

My heart swooped. *Me too*, I thought. *Me too.*

"But sometimes it takes people longer to find their right path in life." She turned and looked me straight in the eye. "Carl wasn't ever the right man for you."

The mention of his name didn't make my heart flutter in anticipation anymore. It didn't create the same creeping feeling of dread that I'd worn like a cloak for the last twelve months. I'd more than accepted he was gone—I was grateful for it. "I know. It took me a while to see it, but I'm better off for him leaving."

Ivy nodded. "It leaves room for someone else to come into your life."

At the moment, all I could see in that space was Sebastian, but I knew that would fade. *Wouldn't it?* I'd have to work hard to rub away the oh-so-vivid images he'd left behind. But I wasn't going to be a woman who waited around for a fantasy. There had been nothing *fake* between Sebastian and me, but it had been *fleeting*. I'd always known that.

"You need someone who sees what a kind, generous, lovely girl you are. And you're still a girl. To me at least. You have your entire life ahead of you."

"Thanks, Ivy. I feel a lot better than I did this time last year."

"Sebastian going hasn't brought to the surface all that nasty business with Carl?"

A shiver raced up my spine. Had she known all along? I shook my head. "Your grandson is a special man and a good friend. But I have no expectations there."

Ivy laughed, long and throaty. "Well, that makes one of us. I'd have loved to have seen you two together." She took a sip of her almost-cold chocolate. "Sebastian takes a while to see what's right in front of him. Look how long it took him to come back to Snowsly."

"Well, no offense to Sebastian, but this woman isn't waiting around for him to catch up. I've been that girl. I waited six years for a proposal from Carl and I won't make that mistake again. I want to build my own life, have my own desires and ambitions. Then, if the right man comes along who shares my vision and wants to join me on that journey, we'll see if there's a path forward for us. For now, I'm in the right place with the right people."

Ivy gave one slow nod. "Sounds like you've done a lot of growing up in the last year."

I grinned, thinking back to the memory of that first kiss with Sebastian, of the night in Snowsville, of the burning ritual. "All any of us can do is keep moving forward. And keep striving toward happiness. Which reminds me, can I accept your kind Christmas lunch invitation?" I'd been putting off accepting because I really didn't know how I was going to feel celebrating after what had happened last year. But Sebastian had made sure I'd moved on and that I wanted to celebrate this year, no matter what had happened last.

"I'd be delighted to have you. There will be a whole gang of people. I say, the more the merrier."

A merry Christmas was almost guaranteed in Snowsly. A merry Christmas at Snowsly Manor was an absolute certainty. It was just a shame that the man who'd shared my bed recently wouldn't be sitting next to me.

TWENTY-FIVE

Celia

I stepped out of the Manor and into the frigid night air. I pulled my Christmas tree hat down so low I could barely see. Maybe it would snow tonight. That would go some way to making up for not having Sebastian here tomorrow.

The Christmas market was in full swing and the smell of cinnamon and roasting chestnuts wafted their way up the hill to the Manor entrance. It was like living in a Hallmark movie. Except this year, there was no happy ending.

A car pulled up just as I started to head home and the door opened.

"Celia?" a voice said. A blonde-bobbed head popped out from around the door, followed by a squeal. "Celia!"

Was I hallucinating? "Lemon?"

I barely kept my balance as my best friend launched herself at me, wrapping her entire body around me. I joined in the squealing. "I can't believe you're here!" I said as the driver of Lemon's car approached, carrying a suitcase.

"Inside, miss?"

Lemon peeled herself off me and nodded. "Yes please."

"You're not staying with me?" I asked. What was happening? How was she here and I didn't know about it?

"I've got a room booked here. No offense to you, but I'm quite looking forward to staying in a hotel. It's all arranged."

"Since when?" How long had she been keeping this from me?

"Since Sebastian called me two days ago and offered to fly me over."

I stopped breathing and the blood slowed in my veins. "He did what?"

"He didn't want you to be alone on Christmas Eve. He tried to get me here earlier—didn't want you sad today—but this was the earliest I could get a flight."

My heart twisted in my chest. Sebastian was such a good man. Even though I hadn't known him long, I knew he was special. Special to me. "I can't believe it."

"Seems like a good guy."

We headed back into the Manor, nudging each other like over-excited teenagers.

I sighed. "I know. Did I tell you he bought me a car?"

Lemon burst out laughing. "A car? Like, to keep?"

"It's ludicrous, really. I should never have accepted it, but he said my other car wasn't safe and he wanted to keep me safe and . . . and I don't think I could ever say no to him."

The more time I spent with Sebastian, the more I realized that the grief I'd experienced over the last twelve months hadn't been about Carl at all. My sadness had been for the future I thought I was going to have, the "certainty" that Sebastian had pointed out was just an illusion, and a complete lack of direction. I'd bobbed along this last year without knowing where I was going to end up. Carl leaving brought the curtain up on a pile of things I should have been thinking about while he was still in my life. What did I want? Who did I want to be?

"You think a car is great—I haven't even told you that he flew me business class. It's only fair to let you know that this will be my last trip over to see you. There's no way I can afford to fly business again, but there's no way I can go back to flying economy. Like, ever again."

"You got used to the high life quickly, I see."

"Absolutely. I'm going to have to win the lottery or rob a bank or something. Or maybe one of my business ideas will take off." Lemon was always having business ideas. I had no doubt that one day, she'd be as successful as she'd always dreamed.

When Lemon was all checked in, we kicked off our shoes and clambered onto the bed in the Blue Room. "This was where Sebastian was staying," I said, glancing around. "It's nice."

"You want to smell a pillow or something? I don't mind."

I laughed. "No, maybe later."

"Let's raid the mini bar." Lemon scooted off the bed and grabbed two miniature bottles of Baileys. "This seems festive."

"Reminds me of how we used to steal it from your parents' kitchen cupboard."

"It's like liquid chocolate. It's so stupid that they make it. It's dangerous."

"How long are you here for?" I asked. "We're going to have to pace ourselves on the celebrating."

"Ten days. Technically work thinks I'm just off until New Year's Day, but they don't know I'll be calling in sick because I'll still be here. And before I leave, we're burning that Star Wars duvet cover, even if I have to break into your house and steal the damn thing."

"Actually, there's no need. I burned it already. Sebastian and I had a . . . ritual of a sort." My insides warmed at the memory of the warmth of Sebastian's hand in mine as we watched Carl's things go up in smoke. He was right—the anger that I'd been pushing down was out, and I felt lighter now. Ready for anything.

"You did? Sounds like Sebastian knows exactly what's good for you."

"In more ways that you need to know." I grinned at the thought of our countless hours in bed. "I'm so happy you're here."

"And sad Sebastian isn't?" she asked.

"I keep telling myself to be logical. I always knew he lived in London and that we were just a short-term thing . . . It's just, I really like him. Sure, he was handsome and tall and seemed to be able to snap his fingers and get just about anything he wanted. But he was also kind and loyal and incredibly humble. He always played down his contributions to the village."

"Sounds like someone else I know," Lemon said. "But seriously, there must have been something wrong with him. Did he have a tiny penis?"

I shook my head. "Sorry to disappoint you. I think he might just be the perfect man. For me." Carl was hard to get over because of what he represented. But Sebastian was going to be hard to get over because of who he was.

At least this Christmas, when life handed me lemons, it also handed me Lemon. I was so grateful to have her here with me—once again, thanks to Sebastian. He'd fixed things for a final time before he left.

TWENTY-SIX

Sebastian

I'd made this walk along Delphinium Row at least twenty times over the last fortnight, but tonight my heart was beating out of my chest as if I'd run straight from the M40. I couldn't wait to see what pajamas she was wearing, what Christmas music was playing in the cottage, and whether or not she'd be happy to see me.

In the middle of Celia's front door, there was just enough wood not obstructed by Christmas wreath for me to knock.

I waited.

And waited.

And waited.

Gradually my heartbeat faded back to normal and I gave one last knock before I shoved my hands deep in my pockets. Where was she?

I'd asked Bradley to drop me off here while he drove up to the Manor and left my case before heading home to his own family. On the journey back from the motorway, I'd ordered a rental car to be delivered on Boxing Day so I was never forced back into a Mini again. I'd taken it for ten days. I wasn't sure I was going to spend all that time in Snowsly, but I wasn't ready to say exactly when I was going back to London, either.

Maybe tonight if Celia didn't open her front door.

Perhaps someone in the village was having a Christmas Eve party I didn't know about. And then I remembered; Lemon had arrived. I'd arranged for her to stay at the Manor. I turned, trying to decide what to do and where to go next, when I saw a figure turn into the row. The flashing lights on her head told me it was Celia. She was humming a Christmas song and scuffing up the three-day-old snow with her boots.

And then she looked up. She stopped walking and pulled her eyebrows together. "Sebastian?"

"I like your hat." I nodded toward the knitted Christmas tree stretched across her head, its lights flashing on and off. "Are you battery operated?"

"What are you doing here?" Disappointingly, she completely ignored my hat jibe.

She started toward me. I walked back up the pathway to meet her.

"I know you don't like Christmas Eve goodbyes. So I thought I'd say hello instead." There was nothing I'd prefer to be doing than gazing at Celia and her ludicrous hat right now. Not even sipping whisky in first class on the way to the Caribbean.

"What about your flight?" A smile unraveled on her face and I tried and failed to keep mine under wraps.

"I suppose it's going without me. I decided that it was about time I had a Christmas in Snowsly."

We stood toe to toe either side of the thigh-high gate.

"Oh, and thank you, Secret Santa," I said. "I appreciated your gifts. Very you, but at the same time, very me."

"You sent me Lemon." Her eyes went glassy and she shook her head. "It's hands-down the nicest thing anyone's ever done for me. Thank you."

"It was a pleasure. You deserve a wonderful Christmas."

"I'd kiss you if I didn't think it would be the last thing I did before I froze to death."

Celia looked skyward and instinctively I did the same. "It's snowing," she said. "Another Christmas miracle." She laughed one of her joyously unselfconscious laughs and pulled out her keys. "I better get you a hot chocolate since you've sacrificed a holiday in Barbados."

"Oh, I wouldn't say it was much of a sacrifice." How much had changed in the last fourteen days?

We headed inside and unwrapped ourselves from layers of hats, coats, scarves, jumpers, and boots. "I drove my new car earlier for the first time. It's like being in a Rolls freaking Royce. Did I tell you that a friend bought me a car for Christmas?"

I followed her into the kitchen. "A friend? Or a boyfriend?" I pulled out the chair in the kitchen that I usually sat on while she made us drinks, while I waited for her to answer.

Eventually she turned to face me. "I'm not sure. I know I like him. And he seems to like me—"

"Very much," I interrupted.

"But life isn't so straightforward. There are . . . obstacles."

I released the chair and stalked toward her, circling her waist with my arms, unable to resist touching her for another second. "You and I have become pretty good at overcoming obstacles these last weeks. If you tell me what we're facing, I think we can figure out a way through them."

She softened in my arms and smoothed her hands over my chest. "You think?" The wrinkle between her eyebrows told me she wasn't so sure.

"I know so. Let's whip up the hot chocolate and go through it. Break it down. Find solutions."

She laughed. "Seriously? We live in different parts of the country," she said, pulling out of my arms and turning toward the work surface to start on our drinks. "You can't do whatever it is you do in Snowsly. And I don't want to leave this place. That seems like a pretty big obstacle. You haven't been back here for ten years."

"That was a mistake," I said.

She put the kettle on and leaned on the counter, folding her arms as if she wasn't to be proved wrong.

We'd see about that.

"It's thirty minutes in a helicopter. And I own my business. I can work from home one or two days a week. Maybe more sometimes."

She glanced up at me from under her eyelashes. "You're saying you want to make Snowsly your home?"

"I think it always has been. I've just been wandering around looking for it for an awful long time."

"So you want to split your time between London and Snowsly?"

"Plenty of people do it. Half of the Cotswolds is inhabited by people who work in London."

She rolled her eyes. "Not in Snowsly." Some villages were full of commuters and holiday lets, but Celia was right as usual—Snowsly was for lifetime residents.

"But it's possible to make that life work."

"Possible," she replied. "But is it something you want?"

Could she really doubt it? I was supposed to be on a plane to Barbados right now. I'd come back for her.

"I want you." I unfolded her arms and cupped her head in my hands. "I want to do whatever it takes to be with you." I rested my forehead against hers and she sank into my touch, sliding her arms around my waist.

"It's too much to even wish for," she whispered. "I was so desperate for a perfect Christmas, but this year has exceeded all my expectations. Because of you. Even if you hadn't come back, spending these fourteen days before Christmas with you would have made it the best Christmas I've ever had."

Thank God she felt the same as I did.

"We've just got wrinkles to iron out. That's all. But I like you. Very much. And I don't want this to be the only Christmas we spend together." We hadn't known each other very long, but I'd never felt so comfortable, so connected, so completely myself with anyone like I did with Celia. I'd spent my life working in an industry where everyone was trying to pretend they were a little more than who they were in order to secure a new job.

Celia knew she was enough.

And I didn't need anything else.

"Are you sure you're ready for Christmas with me?" She pulled back to look at me. "You thought I was festive before, but you're in for a treat."

"If I'm with you, I know that's true."

She tilted her head. "Same."

Something deep in my gut told me that this Christmas with her would be the first of many. Next year, when my mother would join us. Another when we might get engaged.

A Christmas wedding. Celia posing in front of the Manor tree with our first baby in her arms. There was a lifetime of wonderful Christmas memories waiting for us. Looking into Celia's ice-blue eyes, I could tell she knew it too.

TWENTY-SEVEN

Sebastian

It was Christmas morning and I'd just woken up, but I could tell, even though the lights were off and Celia had her back to me in bed, that something was wrong. I reached for her and pulled her against me. "What is it?"

She sighed in my arms. "I haven't made a stocking for you. I don't have a single present."

Relief jettisoned through my body. "I don't need anything. And anyway, you weren't expecting me. Don't get hung up on this, Celia. Today is perfect because we're together, not because we've bought each other gifts."

"But I want to do gifts. They're important to me."

"We have plenty of Christmases ahead of us for gifts. Let's just enjoy today."

She bolted upright. "And I've said yes to Christmas lunch at the Manor. I can't leave Lemon on her own, but I don't want to leave you here?"

I groaned and turned onto my back. "I called Granny last night. She's expecting me for lunch too."

She snapped her head back to look at me. "You did? That's even better. We can spend the day together, but with everyone."

"I told you. You and I overcome obstacles. We figure it out. You don't need to worry."

She fell back onto the mattress. "I think you might be right." She turned to me and kissed me on the lips. I pulled her closer.

"Holy shit," she screamed, pulling out of my arms and leaping out of bed. "It's half past eleven."

Now it was my turn to bolt out of bed. "We're due at the Manor at twelve. We have time."

"I don't want to miss the pre-dinner charades," she said.

I chuckled. "Yep, definitely don't want to miss that."

She shoved me playfully as she passed me to go to the bathroom. "I mean it. This is going to be part of our annual traditions. Maybe Lemon being here will be one as well." She reached for my face. "You are my favorite person on earth for bringing her here."

"Griffin too. I invited him on my way back to Snowsly last night. He's arriving by helicopter, so we should hear him when he gets here."

Celia froze, then slowly turned toward me with eyes wide as Christmas baubles.

"What?" I asked. "You're going to love Griffin. He's a bit flash but he's got a great heart."

She nodded and I could tell she was cycling through ideas in her head. "Do you think *Lemon* will like Griffin?"

I chuckled. Oh, *that's* what she was thinking. I shrugged. "I've never met Lemon. And neither has Griffin. Shall we give it twenty-four hours before you start match-making? Especially when we have twenty-five minutes to get up to the Manor."

She squealed and bolted for the bathroom.

I caught her wrist and pulled her back to me. "Are you sure you don't want to start a tradition where we just stay in bed all day?"

She pulled free. "Absolutely not, but we can talk about starting some kind of Boxing Day tradition that involves a lot of sex. But Christmas Day? We're going to play games, eat and drink too much and watch the Queen's speech with our friends and Snowsly family."

And with that declaration, she stomped into the bathroom.

We got to the Manor at exactly midday, a box of crackers under my arm, ready for proceedings to begin. I wasn't exactly nervous, but I wasn't exactly not nervous either. This was it. My first Snowsly Christmas. I'd waited a hell of a long time for this and there was still a part of me reluctant to live the reality. Perhaps I was concerned I'd be disappointed or worse, I'd realize how much I'd lost all these years. It hadn't happened so far, but there was still time.

"Sebastian and Celia," Granny said, beaming up at the two of us as we entered the living room. On the sofas, Barbara, Howard, Keely, and Jim were all settled with what looked like sherry in their hands. Carols played in the background and the fire was crackling in the fireplace, filling the room with the scent of pine. The tree by the window seemed to have more lights on it than usual. So this was what Christmas Day was meant to be like. I had no idea why I'd stayed away so long.

"We brought crackers." Celia nudged me and I handed them over. "I made them," she said.

"Thank you," Granny said. "Everyone has to contribute if you come to my Christmas Day at the Manor. Howard has made sure the firewood is well stocked. Barbara has cooked her infamous Christmas pudding, Jim provided the music and Keely brought her stuffing, Celia brought the crackers and I've tried to perfect the tablescape." I glanced across at Granny's dining table over by the tree, which had been transformed into a Christmas village, complete with ski slope and miniature figures creakily moving downhill. "I got so carried away, I think we'll have to eat in the Manor dining room. But that's by the by." Granny fixed me with a warm look. "Oh yes, and Lemon is in the kitchen making . . ." A concerned expression crossed her face. "Something involving sweet potatoes and marshmallow." She lowered her voice. "Sounds utterly disgusting but I'm trying to remain open-minded."

"Since we didn't know you'd be joining us, Sebastian, I haven't allocated you anything. I suggest you give a little toast." She nodded toward the two outstanding glasses on Mary's tea tray that had been pushed up against the side of the sofa. "I chilled some port for you, Sebastian. I know you're not a sherry drinker."

Granny had thought of everything.

"Absolutely," I said, picking up the two glasses and handing one to Celia. Her eyes went wide before she took a seat next to Barbara.

I cleared my throat. "I'm honored to spend my first Christmas at Snowsly this year among the finest people I've ever met—"

The door to Granny's sitting room swung open and Griffin appeared, grinning from ear to ear and wearing a Santa hat. "Ho, ho, ho," he said. "I've brought the champers." He was carrying a large box which he half-dropped, half-placed on the floor.

"Welcome, Griffin," Granny said. "It's nice to meet you finally."

Just then, Lemon—also wearing a Santa hat—appeared in the doorway behind Griffin.

Griffin turned to greet her. "Mrs. Claus?"

"Santa!" she said, as if a man in a Santa hat calling her Mrs. Claus was just what she'd been expecting. "I've just put the sweet potato casserole in the oven."

"And Griffin bought champagne," Granny said. "Now we just have Sebastian's speech and we can seat ourselves at the table. Sebastian?"

"As I was saying, I'm delighted and honored to spend my first Christmas at Snowsly this year among the finest people I've ever met. We—I'd like to think I'm one of you now—have had the most successful Christmas market ever. We've overcome every obstacle put in our way." My eyes slid to Celia, who blushed under my gaze. For the first time since I'd met her, she wore her hair loose. It fell across her shoulders in rivulets of glossy white icicles. Her ice-blue eyes burned bright.

"But I can't be sorry for any of the issues we faced. Granny's ankle brought me here, the tree falling down brought the village together, and getting stranded overnight in Snowsville . . . Well, let's just say it all worked out in the end. We stayed on course and stayed true to what Snowsly is: a family." I raised my glass. "To Snowsly."

Everyone joined in with my toast. "To Snowsly," they cheered in unison.

"Thank you, Sebastian," Granny replied. "And I know you say it's a group effort, and of course it is, but I wanted to say special thanks for coming when I called."

"There's nothing I wouldn't do for you, Granny."

I hadn't been prepared to stay in Snowsly for Christmas Day, not at first. But Granny's continued love and commitment to me and my happiness meant that when I finally changed my mind, I was welcomed as if I'd spent every Christmas here since I was born.

I sat on the arm of the sofa next to Celia, leaned over and clinked my glass against hers.

"I know we shouldn't say this, Sebastian," Barbara said, "but we've all been rooting for you two since . . . well, honestly, since this time last year."

I chuckled at the thought of Celia becoming single and the villagers of Snowsly planning her next relationship with a man none of them had seen for ten years. But then again, maybe they'd been on to something.

"Yes," Howard said. "I always thought you two would be a good match."

The last two weeks had felt like a lifetime. Not because it had been difficult, but because they seemed to erase all the time before. This was where I should have been all along. This was home.

"I knew he'd be back one day," Barbara said. "We've missed you."

Celia threaded her fingers through mine and I squeezed her hand. "I've missed you too." Without ever knowing her, I'd even sort of missed Celia, or at least, there was something inside me that I hadn't known was empty until it was suddenly satiated. I'd found who I'd been looking for, exactly where I was meant to be.

EPILOGUE

Later on that day

Sebastian

Christmas Day in Snowsly was pretty much like any other day in Snowsly. Full of kindness, laughter, and that sense of home I'd been missing for so long. How could I have thought I might have been disappointed by being here?

Granny had catered for twenty-five rather than fifteen, but she insisted that leftovers were actually more important that the actual Christmas lunch.

"I've done my best," Howard said, putting his knife and fork down and rubbing his belly. "I just can't eat another morsel. That Christmas pudding was magnificent, Barbara. It always is."

Barbara blushed at Howard's compliment and I couldn't help but wonder if anything romantic had happened between them. Maybe the port or the champagne was getting to me. Or maybe it was just the festive season making me soft. More likely it was because I wanted everyone to be as happy as I was.

"Thank you, Sebastian, for flying me over," Lemon said. "And thank you, Ivy, for having me for lunch."

"It's delightful to have you with us," Granny said. "And you, Griffin."

It was good to have Griffin here. It was fitting. We'd spent almost every Christmas together since we were eighteen together.

Lunch had been delicious and Celia's crackers a triumph. Each cracker contained a handmade Christmas decoration, which everyone loved. And I was going to be sure to smuggle some pigs in blankets back to the cottage with me when we left. Maybe I'd even grab another slice of Christmas pudding.

"Sebastian, my darling boy, I want to show you something. Will you help me out around the back?" Granny pushed herself up from where she sat at the head of the table.

"Shall I grab your Zimmer frame?"

"No need. I'm feeling much better now."

I frowned. "Maybe a walking stick. You don't want to—"

"Sebastian," Granny groaned at me.

I got to my feet and pressed a kiss onto Celia's head, ignoring the resultant *aww* from Barbara.

"Now that our plan has worked and you two are an item, can we start playing 'Last Christmas' again?" Howard asked. "It's my favorite Christmas tune and I've missed it this year."

An awkward silence settled on the table.

"Every time that song started up, it jumped to the next track," I said. "That was deliberate?"

Keely shrugged and Barbara cleared her throat. I

glanced around at the rest of the table who seemed to be finding their empty plates incredibly interesting.

"We were just trying to make this year less painful for Celia," Granny said. "Now, come on, follow me—"

"That's very sweet of you," Celia said. "And much appreciated, but what was that thing you said Howard, about your plan had worked now that Sebastian and I were an *item*?"

"Oh, he's just drunk," Granny said. "Can you lend me your arm, will you?"

I shook my head. "I think you might have some explaining to do."

"Nothing to explain at all," said Granny. "Like we've all said before, we all thought you two would be a perfect match. And now you are."

I growled, unconvinced that we were getting the whole story, but Celia patted my hand and I let it go. I'd get the truth out of Granny at some point.

"Are you sure I can't just get you whatever you need?" I asked.

"Yes I am," Granny said. "Follow me."

I glanced back at Celia as I followed Granny out of the sitting room. Celia looked so happy. So content. So completely gorgeous. I was a lucky man.

"Should you really be walking this much?" I asked as we turned back on ourselves and Granny grabbed a coat and scarf from the rack. "We're not going outside, are we?"

"Not for long. Follow me," she said.

I didn't understand why we had to do anything straight after lunch. But I wasn't about to argue with Granny. I grabbed my coat and slid it on as we headed outside.

The rush of cold air hit my body like a brick wall. It had

been so cozy around the dining table. Why did we have to leave, and for the frigid outdoors of all places?

She maneuvered with ease over the stone patio and across to the waist-high wall that marked the edge of the gardens of the Manor and the start of the fields and farmland that she'd been leasing out as pasture land for as long as I could remember.

"You see this field," she said, nodding toward the adjacent property. The grass was covered in a sheet of icy frosting. The animals that normally fed here were tucked up, warm in one of Fred's barns.

"Yes, you still renting it out as pasture for Fred's cows?"

"Not for years. Too disruptive for guests and anyway, it's too close to the village. The cows used to get startled by the guests wanting photographs."

"So it's just been empty?"

"Not exactly. I've had . . . wheels in motion. And a couple of months ago, I got this." She pulled out some papers I hadn't noticed tucked under her arm.

"Not an offer for sale?" I asked, taking the papers from her. The farmland around the Manor meant that views were unobstructed and guaranteed to stay that way. If she needed the money, I could give her whatever she wanted.

She didn't answer, but nodded, urging me to open the papers.

There were about fifteen pages of formal-looking documents and plans, and then something on the top right-hand corner caught my attention. *Outline Planning Permission.*

"Oh and the document at the back," she said, indicating another set of papers.

It read *Deed of Transfer*, and had my name at the top.

"Granny, what's happening?"

"It's your Christmas present. But only if you want it.

You've got five years to decide whether you want to build. That's how long the outline planning permission lasts."

"Planning permission for what?"

"A family home," she said simply. As if she'd just announced she was getting new cushions for the sofa. "I know you love your life in London, but sometimes you need a place that takes you away. And now, you and Celia—you might want a place in the village."

Then it struck me what was happening. She was giving me the field. A place to build a home. "Granny," I said, unable to find the right words.

"Like I say, you might not want to build anything. In which case, congratulations you got given a shitty field for Christmas, but—"

"It's perfect. And Celia and I—she's a special woman from a special place, and I'm planning to spend a lot more time in Snowsly. To be with her. With you. To be home."

Granny pressed her palm to her chest. "You're a darling boy. You know you're always welcome at the Manor, but . . ."

"But now I get to build my own home. And I get to be next door to you."

She glanced up at me. "Is that okay?"

I pulled her into a hug, being careful not to knock her off her feet. "It's more than okay. It's the best present I could have hoped for."

"You've always had a place to call home in Snowsly. And you always will."

"Thank you, Granny."

"Thank you for making me so proud."

Snowsly was like one of those friends that you hadn't seen since school but picked up like you'd seen them yester-

day. It was constant. Familiar. It was everything I needed
from the place I wanted to call home.

It was almost midnight by the time we got back to
Delphinium Row from the Manor. I finally let go of Celia
so we could get through the gate.

"I'm surprised our breath didn't freeze in the air and
then fall to the ground and shatter," she said. "It's so cold."

"You know we need hot chocolate."

She unlocked the door and I followed her as quickly as
possible so I didn't let any more cold air in than I had to.

"Or sex," she said, checking her watch. "By the time
we've gotten all these layers off, it will technically be Boxing
Day."

"And Boxing Day is now officially Sex Day?" I toed off
my boots and unbuttoned my coat.

"Sex and Leftovers Day. Though preferably not at the
same time." Celia pulled off her Santa hat and hung it on
the coat hook, like she might get one more wear out of it
tomorrow. It was going to be Sex Day, after all.

I wasn't sure I'd heard of anything so bloody fantastic.
Cold pigs in blankets and sex with Celia? I might have died
and gone to heaven. "Oh, and there's something else we
need to do."

Celia turned to me, scrunching up her nose in protest.

"I'm hoping you're going to be excited." I pulled out the
papers from my inside pocket, hung my coat on the hook,
and then followed Celia into the kitchen. "Granny gave me
the meadow next to the Manor, and all the necessary
permissions to build a house."

"You're going to build a house?"

I nodded. "In Snowsly."

We had talked about logistics of me juggling my work in London with being in Snowsly, but we hadn't talked about where I was going to live. It was still early days in my relationship with Celia, but there was no need to prevaricate. The house I wanted to build on the meadow was for *us*.

"I thought we could think about what we might like that house to look like. Number of bedrooms, whether we want a formal dining room, an orangery, that sort of thing."

She tilted her head. "What *we* want the house to look like. Isn't that up to you?"

I tossed the papers on the dining table and pulled her toward me. "I hope it will be *our* house. That we'll live there together when it's done."

She glanced around at the kitchen as if she was considering whether or not she was prepared to give it up. An instant later, her face lit up in a smile. "Yeah, I think I'd like that. On one condition."

"Name it." I'd take her on whatever terms she offered.

"I get to go full throttle Santa's grotto on the Christmas decorations."

"I would be disappointed with anything less."

This year's festive season wasn't at all how I'd pictured. It had been a thousand times better. I was already looking forward to next Christmas. With Celia. In our new home. In Snowsly.

Three months later

Celia

A fizzle of excitement bloomed in my chest as I glanced around Ivy's sitting room at Howard, Barbara, Jim, Keely,

Ivy, and of course, Sebastian. "It's so good to see everyone," I said.

Howard frowned. "You see us all the time. I said hello to you this morning when I was out for milk and yesterday when you were walking across the green and—"

"I know, I just mean, it's good to be meeting as a committee again," I said. "It means Christmas isn't that far away."

"It's March," Sebastian barked. "The spring equinox to be exact. Christmas is almost as far away as it can be."

I couldn't dampen down my grin even if I wanted to. I enjoyed this grumpy side to Sebastian as much as I enjoyed the joyful side and his downright sexy side.

We only had nine months to plan for Christmas. We had to focus.

"First order of business," Ivy said. "Lemon and Griffin. Lovely people. What are we thinking?"

"I like them," Jim said.

"That Griffin is a very funny chap," Barbara said. "And Lemon—her name's absurd of course, but she's lovely, and they seem very well suited."

Was I missing something? We were here to talk about planning for next year's Christmas. Why were we talking about mine and Sebastian's best friends?

"I'm sorry, but why are we talking about Lemon and Griffin? This is a Christmas committee meeting that I've been dragged along to. Shouldn't we be discussing Christmas?"

"We are," Keely said, with a gently scolding look to Sebastian. "Bringing people together is a key thing at Christmas. Creating happiness and wonder."

"It's what we do," said Howard. "Look at you two."

I glanced at Ivy and then at Sebastian. "Yes, Sebastian

and I are very happy. But we weren't designed by committee. We found out we liked each other—"

"By spending time together," Ivy said.

"By banding together in a crisis," Barbara added.

"By thinking up solutions to problems together," Jim said.

"Don't forget a trip to Snowsville," Howard said, chortling. "Do you know how long it took me to syphon off the petrol in your tank while you were going around the Snowsville Christmas market? You could have left it half-empty!"

"What?" I yelped. "You drained the petrol from my Mini?"

"We had to find a way of getting you two together. You needed a little push," Ivy said.

It had all been a conspiracy. Sebastian and I had been purposefully put together.

"Granny," Sebastian said with a growl. "Did you even have a sprained ankle?"

She frowned as if she wasn't quite sure how to answer the question. "I have sprained it before. Last summer. Only had to stay off it a couple of days."

"I remember," Howard said. "That's when we thought up our little matchmaking plan."

"The website hack was genius," Keely said. "It really added to the idea that Snowsville was out to get us."

I should be furious about being hoodwinked by these people. Lied to for all these months. But when I gazed up at Sebastian, all I could think was, thank goodness. Whether by fate or interfering neighbors, we had found each other. I had the best man I could ever hope for by my side. I couldn't be angry.

"You lot are incorrigible," Sebastian said. "But all's well that ends well."

Ivy nodded and Keely gave three little claps, like she was happy it was all out in the open.

"Thank you for helping me come to my senses and guiding me to the woman I love."

I blushed at his public declaration. We'd swapped our first *I love yous* a few weeks ago, but I was still getting used to having someone in my life who so obviously adored me. Sebastian told me I had a lifetime to get used to it. He'd also told me not to expect a Christmas Eve proposal. Which was a relief, but at the same time a disappointment. Maybe I should propose to him. That way I wasn't waiting for something that might or might not happen, and I had all the fun in planning it. I might even rope in some of the people in this room if they were so invested in Sebastian and I being together.

"Well now that's all out in the open," Ivy said. "I suggest we take a vote on whether Lemon and Griffin should be the next Snowsly couple in our sights."

Sebastian grinned while shaking his head, but I stretched up my hand as high as it would reach. Lemon deserved a good man just as much as I did. And if it meant her living back in the UK? Well, I wasn't going to complain about having my best friend back in the country.

"Neither of them live in Snowsly," Sebastian said.

"You hadn't been here for ten years," Ivy replied. "We've overcome bigger issues."

"Put your hand up," I whispered.

Sebastian shook his head but raised his hand as requested.

"We have nine months, people, and a lot to do."

A Snowsly Christmas. Another Snowsly couple. And in the meantime, I had a proposal to plan.

To read Griffin and Lemon's story read **This Christmas**

Have you read **Mr. Park Lane**? Read on for a sneak peek.

BOOKS BY LOUISE BAY

The Mister Series

Mr. Mayfair

Mr. Knightsbridge

Mr. Smithfield

Mr. Park Lane

The Christmas Collection

The 14 Days of Christmas

This Christmas

The Player Series

International Player

Private Player

Standalones

Hollywood Scandal

Love Unexpected

Hopeful

The Empire State Series

Gentleman Series

The Wrong Gentleman

The Ruthless Gentleman

Sign up to the Louise Bay mailing list at
www.louisebay/mailinglist

Read more at www.louisebay.com

MR. PARK LANE

Hartford

At twenty-nine, I was a doctor who'd travelled and worked in some of the most deprived places in the world, but just the *thought* of Joshua Luca had me sliding my sweaty palms down my jeans and wishing I could steady my racing heartbeat.

I hadn't seen him in over a decade, but Joshua could still get to me, and I hated it.

It wasn't like we'd ever dated.

It wasn't like I'd been pining for him all these years.

It wasn't like he'd even ever noticed me. Certainly not in the way I'd noticed him.

Joshua had been an almost obsession until, at seventeen, I broke my leg and swore off teenage infatuations for good. In one night, I grew up and let go of my silly crush.

I'd forgotten all those old feelings before my mum announced she'd arranged for me to stay with Joshua for a couple of months until I "found my feet"—unintentional irony, given the cast on my left leg. I didn't argue. It wasn't worth telling her that if I'd figured out living in a war zone, I was pretty sure getting settled in London would be a piece of cake.

Cake. My much-missed friend. Not something there was a lot—or any—of at the Médecins sans frontières outpost in Yemen where I'd been stationed. As soon as I'd dumped my bag and showered, I'd go on the hunt for something lemony. With sprinkles.

I should try to keep my focus on cake. Anything but the memories of Joshua's summer sun-streaked hair. His long, lean, tan legs. The way the dimple in his left cheek would appear whenever my sister was around. His permanent half-smile hinted that he was always in on the joke. And his cool confidence meant that if he ever ended up in trouble, he managed to talk his way into forgiveness. He'd seemed like a god to my teenage self.

I wasn't sure he would remember anything about me. Maybe the unibrow? The braces?

Our parents had been friends since I could remember. Joshua was the same age as my brother. My sister was a year younger, and to my eternal frustration, I was the baby. The baby with a crush on her older brother's best friend.

I was nothing more than a lurking spectator during games of tennis, dares, and talks about girls. Almost like I'd been a part of the scenery—the background in Joshua and my brother's summers. Unlike my older sister, Thea, who'd embraced the denim mini-skirt trend like she was a twenty-five-year old supermodel. Thea was always at the center of everything. I'd watched as she twirled and giggled in front of Joshua, who responded with cocky grins and pouty lips. He'd definitely remember Thea. Unlike forgettable, invisible me.

I'd never told a soul my fantasies about Joshua. And at

seventeen I'd swallowed them down, determined to keep them tucked away in a deep, dark place forever.

Now, as I stood in the airport, about to come face-to-face with him, an unwelcome, familiar shiver breezed across my skin and tripped my pulse.

My phone buzzed. I dipped out of the queue so I didn't breach the mobile ban. It was my mum. I released my right crutch and slid open the phone.

"Have you landed, darling?"

The thing about working in war zones was that your parents always worried. War zones didn't worry me. Reunions did.

"Yep. Will be heading to get my bag in a minute. Can I call you when I get back to Joshua's place?"

"Of course. Marian said it's a wonderful flat. He's such a good boy. Has his own company, a marketing agency. Just bought them a new car, you know."

I must have heard about the new car at least three times. "Yes. The Lexus. I remember." I was never going to be the daughter who bought her parents a brand-new car. I didn't earn that kind of money. And even if I did—they didn't need one.

"He's done very well for himself. Very reliable. I'm sure he'll be waiting for you."

"I could have made it into town on the Heathrow Express." I hated the thought of Joshua going out of his way for me. I was sure he had better things to be doing on a Tuesday than playing chauffeur to me.

"You have a broken leg, Hartford," she said in her you-don't-get-a-say tone. As soon as I'd told my parents I was coming back to London, my mother had pushed her perpetual interfering into a higher gear. I knew it was an expression of her relief. After three years abroad, I'd be a couple of hours away instead of a couple of time zones. Now I was back, I'd have to get better at dodging her well-intentioned help bombs.

I glanced over my shoulder at the wave of people herding down the corridor, heading for the queue. A flight must have just landed, and I didn't want to be stuck behind them all. "I shouldn't keep him waiting. I'll call you later."

"Send my love to Joshua and call me when you've settled in."

There was my icebreaker with Joshua. I could tell him I'd spoken to my mother and she sent her love.

I re-joined the queue and told myself if I could handle treating sick kids on folding beds in searing heat, I could handle Joshua Luca.

No. Big. Deal.

The doors out onto the landside concourse slid open. I scanned the audience of cab drivers with signs and people waiting for loved ones to appear. Set back from the crowd, as if a spotlight was positioned over him, Joshua stood, leaning against a post, head down, focused on his phone.

A fizzle of desire bloomed in my chest. I had to remind myself to breathe. He was still gorgeous. And I was furious about it. I'd set down my torch for Joshua a long time ago and wasn't about to pick it back up. It could only lead to trouble. Again.

His shoulders had broadened, but the dirty blond hair still had a way of looking perfectly tousled. And that magnetic confidence? It was still palpable from ten meters away.

He glanced up and right at me, as if he could hear me thinking. I felt his lopsided smile between my legs.

Vagina, you're a traitor.

I grinned and started toward him as if I'd just been searching him out in the crowd, rather than drawn to him like lightning to a metal rod.

"Hey." I tipped my head back to meet his gaze.

He took his time and made a slow, unapologetic sweep of my body from head to toe and back again, lingering on my lips and my cheeks on the way back. "Hartford?"

Should we kiss? One cheek or two? Hug? Why did I feel so awkward?

Twenty-nine, I reminded myself.

A doctor.

A crush on Joshua Luca leads to nothing but trouble.

I pulled him into a one-handed hug, pushing myself up awkwardly onto a one-legged tiptoe so I could reach around his neck. He stiffened almost unnoticeably before hugging me back.

"Good to see you," I said into his hairline.

I could feel his large hand through my jacket span almost the entire width of my back. And that smell? I'd forgotten that. What was it, and how had it not changed in all these years?

Without asking, he pulled my backpack from me like it weighed nothing and slung it over his shoulder. "That's it? No more luggage?"

I shrugged. "Nope. Just me."

He nodded toward the exit and I followed him. "What happened to your leg?"

I glanced down at my cast as if I needed to clarify which leg he was talking about. "Oh nothing. Just an accident." I didn't want to get into it. I just wanted it to heal.

Quickly. So I could get back to work. "Tell me about you, Joshua Luca. What have you been doing since I last saw you?"

He shot me another trademark smile. "When was the last time I saw you?"

"I can't remember . . ." I knew exactly. I refused to think about what had come after my accident. For years afterward, I ruminated about the night I broke my leg. Joshua had come to collect my brother before heading out to celebrate the New Year. He was in his second year at university and had just turned twenty. As I'd watched him from the top of the stairs, I'd never been so aware of our age difference thanks to the new stubble on his jaw and the flat, toned stomach he unintentionally revealed when he'd reached for my brother's jacket. He'd turned into a man and I still felt like a child. My glimpse of him had lasted thirty seconds max, but it was etched in my memory like a tattoo. Those few seconds had been the last good memories I had of Joshua.

"You lost your braces."

Of course he would remember those.

"Shocking, isn't it? I thought I was going to have to wear them forever. I also tweezed my monobrow. And I got a couple of degrees along the way." People could change. I wasn't who I'd been back then. "It's been a while."

"Right." He glanced over at me and furrowed his brow before looking away. "This is us."

He pressed a button on his key fob and the boot opened on an expensive-looking car. He slung my backpack in before heading the wrong direction to the passenger seat.

And then he opened the door. The passenger door. For me.

I shook my head. Had he grown up in the fifties? It was

all part and parcel of that Joshua Luca charm he'd had since he came out of the womb. I wanted nothing to do with it.

"What?" He looked genuinely confused.

"I can open my own door," I said as I hobbled into the vehicle, pulled my crutches with me, and settled into a buttery leather seat. I wasn't going to be reduced to a melting mess by a small act of chivalry. Not that he was *trying* to make me melt. He didn't see me like that. Joshua didn't have to *try* to make women melt.

Joshua shrugged and shut the door before moving around to the driver's side.

"Sorry if I smell like Yemen. You might need an air freshener in here after our journey."

He pulled out of the parking space and we started twirling through the narrow passages of the multi-story car park. "Yemen? I thought you flew in from Saudi Arabia."

"No direct flights from Yemen."

"Should you be going to places that don't have direct flights?"

I laughed. "You sound like Patrick. I was working with Médecins sans frontières. I wasn't on holiday. But I appreciate the big-brother vibe."

"Right," he said, that frown appearing again. "You want a water?" He pulled open the lid to what looked like a built-in cool box under the arm rest between us and took out a bottle.

"Thanks. You got any cake in there?"

"This isn't Tesco, but you might find an apple."

"I haven't had an apple for thirteen months." I scrambled about and found an apple as green as I'd ever seen. "You want a bite?" I held up the fruit then abruptly pulled it away as my imagination offered up an image of him sinking his teeth into . . . me.

Was he a biter? For a split second, filthy images reeled through my brain: Joshua in bed, naked. Joshua over me, arms flexed and gaze trained on my lips. His hips pushing—

Stop.

I needed to get a grip, buy some brain bleach and dose the butterflies in my stomach with propofol. I was going to be living with this guy for a couple of months. I couldn't be following him around, drooling like some teenager with a crush. Besides, I knew that an obsession over Joshua was dangerous. Literally. I needed to construct an impenetrable Joshua Luca forcefield around myself.

This was strictly a friend zone.

———

I didn't know where to look first: the amazing one-hundred-and-eighty-degree view toward the Millennium Wheel, the ginormous living room with sofas that looked like gooey marshmallow, or that pesky dimple in Joshua's left cheek that had had me hypnotized since I was twelve.

"This is where you live?" I asked, trying to pretend I hadn't noticed the dimple. "You have exceptionally good taste for someone whose greatest childhood pleasure was giving my brother wedgies when he least expected it. It looks like a huge hotel room."

He shoved his hands into his pockets and his gaze hit the floor in exactly the same way as when he used to flirt with Thea. He managed to combine confidence with bashfulness in a way I'd always found completely adorable. Joshua didn't have a shy bone in his body, and I wondered when exactly he realized how sexy a little humility can be. "I can't take credit for the decoration. It's residences of the Park Lane International."

"Residences? As in, you live in a flat that's part of a hotel? You can order room service whenever you like? And use the gym and stuff?"

"And stuff," he confirmed, nodding.

"Wow." I'd spent the previous year sleeping under canvas on a fold-up bed. Five-star luxury was going to take some getting used to. Except I wasn't about to get used to it. I glanced around, trying to see where I might put my things. There only seemed to be one door. Maybe I was on the sofa. "Where am I sleeping?"

"The oven? The bath?" Joshua grinned. "Or maybe the bed in the bedroom? It's a conventional choice but definitely the most comfortable."

Joshua towered above me, his chest wider and broader than it had been when I'd last seen him. He still had the sense of humor of a seventeen-year-old boy. "I'm laughing on the inside. Seriously, Joshua. Which way?"

He shrugged. "I've not been in here before. I'm next door in apartment P1. I guess it's over here." He strode across the living room and pushed open a door. "Yep. This is the bedroom."

"Wait, you don't live in this flat? I thought I was coming to stay in your spare bedroom."

"You hoping to see me in my boxers in the morning?" He grinned and widened his eyes suggestively.

I couldn't deny I'd wondered what Joshua looked like in his boxers in the sixty minutes since we'd left the airport, but I certainly wasn't about to admit to it. "Mum told me you had a spare bedroom."

"This is like the guest bedroom for the penthouse. It's a separate flat that's only available for residents of my place. It's like having a pool house or something."

Decoding the guy-speak, he wanted his own space.

"Joshua, if you didn't want me to stay with you, you just needed to say. I have other friends." I wasn't sure I had that many in London, actually. Most of them were scattered about the country. And the world. But I didn't need Joshua taking pity on me—I could have figured it out. My mother had begged me to stay with him—told me that he was lonely in London and needed the company. Clearly she just wanted to get her own way. Past experience should have been a warning, but I'd been too tired to argue with her and agreed to stay with him until I found a place of my own.

"You're acting like I've asked you to stay in the boot of my car." He was completely unfazed by my reaction. "I got this place for three months. It's no big deal."

"Wait, you rented it for three months?" I couldn't bear to think how much that might be costing. "Return the key. There's no way I can afford—"

Joshua stepped toward me and stroked my arm as if he were trying to tame a wild horse. I tried to ignore the heat, the way his fingers seemed to press into me with authority, the way he smelled so incredible when he was so close.

"It's no big deal. I'm not expecting you to pay for any of it."

I shook off his arm. Physical contact threatened to ignite my old crush like a match to tinder. "Joshua!" He didn't get it at all. "That's even worse. I'm not expecting you to cover my rent. The entire reason you stay in someone's spare room is to avoid incurring the expense at all."

"But *you* don't have the expense. If it makes you feel better, you can pretend it's my spare room."

"I need a shower." I collapsed on the sofa, jetlag, travel, and the last thirteen months catching up with me all at once. I sank into the marshmallow cushions and wondered if I'd ever move again. "Have you paid? Can you get your money back?"

"No. I signed something. And anyway, where else are you going to go? Someone's spare room or worse, a *sofa*, when you can be here?" He nodded toward the view. "You've been off curing the sick in faraway places. You can see this as your reward."

I didn't want praise or thank-yous. "You're ridiculous."

He smirked. "You're welcome. I presume you're hungry." He messed about on his phone. "You haven't turned into one of those do-gooding vegans, have you?"

"Yes, I'm hungry, and no." I'd been dreaming about eating a burger as big as my plaster-covered leg for the last year. Nothing about my fantasy involved vegetables.

"Thank God. Burgers then?"

Despite my irritation with Joshua, a small smile crept across my lips. He might be my exact opposite when it came to lifestyle, but when it came to taste in food, apparently we'd been separated at birth. *And maybe some cake*, I didn't say. I was picky when it came to sponge, and I wanted to be able to take some time deciding on my first post-Yemen piece. "There isn't much I wouldn't do for a burger right now."

"Interesting," he said, sliding a glance at me as he tapped away on his phone. Then he sat down on the sofa opposite. "Maybe I can think of a few things." I wasn't sure how a dimple could be suggestive, but Joshua's managed it.

His bold flirtations had never been directed at me before. It was sort of flattering, but I had to remind myself it was simply how he operated. He didn't know how *not* to flirt. To Joshua, flirting was some kind of unconscious habit, as automated as breathing.

"It's nice to see you haven't changed a bit."

"It's nice to see you have." He paused and for a split second, looked at me like we were long-time lovers rather than virtual strangers. He blinked twice, cleared his throat. "Except the disapproving scowl is still the same."

"Hey," I said, tossing an expensive cushion at him. He batted it away like candy floss. "I don't scowl."

He chuckled. "Don't worry. It's cute."

Cute?

I was going to have to supercharge my forcefield.

Click to read **MORE**

Made in the USA
Las Vegas, NV
20 November 2021